LAY OF THE LAND

ANONYMOUS

Carroll & Graf Publishers, Inc.
New York

Copyright © 1990 by Carroll & Graf Publishers, Inc

First Carroll & Graf edition 1990

Carroll & Graf Publishers, Inc.
260 Fifth Avenue
New York, NY 10001

ISBN: 0-88184-605-8

Manufactured in the United States of America

LAY OF THE LAND

1

This is an important occasion, this beginning of a remarkable Memoir; and Gladys seems to appreciate its full significance. She has a new dress, or rather costume, for the draped confection that does not at all conceal the exquisite curves of her body, undresses rather than dresses her. You must understand what I mean. She would rather have been far less indelicate stark naked, than in this mazy, fluffy cloud which by its half hearted attempt to conceal anything, accentuates the charm of everything.

Delicious arms and legs has Gladys, and the rosy flesh gleams through the transparent drapery; nipples as carmine as her lips, and a waist rounded cleanly as her throat. The gauze ceases at her knees; thence is a dress of black silk stockings and natty patent leather shoes.

Her little fingers, bedecked with costly rings, (we have had more than one wealthy visitor since the beginning of the book) — hover over the keys of the machine. A brimming glass of champagne stands at the elbow of each of us, cigarettes are to hand; in fact, it only needs the word for 'Blanche La Mare' to start her redoubtable career.

I never expected George Reynolds to come back. I knew I was done, and my chances of seeing him again about as remote as the likelihood of recovering the two five pounds notes he had borrowed. As a matter of fact, I minded losing my husband less than the money; his conduct and letter had shown him up a bit too much. I could only damn my own folly in trusting him at all. I was cold and tired there, and the grey dawn accentuated my loneliness. I had hungered for man's society and protection, a man's arms round me, and a man's breast to nestle against; also I had been more than a bit curious to discover what the absolute act of love really was. Many girls in my position would have done the same. That I should have wished to get married puzzled me, for the thought of a life-long bondage had always terrified me. I suppose in the depths of every woman's heart there is an elemental store of puritanism that leads her at times to covet the plain gold ring that can cover such a multitude of sins. Also there is undoubtedly a fascination in the term of husband; to be able to introduce my husband to a yet unwed friend is a privilege for which I am quite sure many a girl has taken the plunge and risked the cares of a household and the misery of children. Well, I had taken the plunge, and had soused myself beyond any possibility of ever getting dry again. Here I was, wedded and yet unwedded, with the world ahead of me, a big black mark against my name for a start, and no maidenhead.

Meanwhile breakfast made its appearance, and

with the warm tea and ham and eggs, confidence came to me, and I began to seriously consider the future and the career I was to adopt. There were very few open to me. I scanned the 'Situations Vacant' columns in the Daily Telegraph, but there wasn't a thing that could possibly suit. That first haven of the homeless girl, governessing, was effectually closed to me.

To begin with I had no references, and secondly, I should have undoubtedly succumbed to the amatory advances of one or other of the male members of whatever family I found myself in, and so taken the mistress's shameful order and the push out. I canvassed the idea of a lady typewriter, but the probable drudgery terrified me; also I should have to learn to type, and very likely buy a machine, which wouldn't have left much of my twenty five pounds. Besides I had heard a typewriter's position in this great metropolis entailed a good deal of sitting on the knees of elderly employers, what time the trousers of the said employers were not at all in their proper decorum. If I was going to lead an immoral career I judged it better to do it on the stage. I had all the advantages of youth and health and one of the best figures in London, so I presumed there ought not be to much difficulty in obtaining a living wage, and so, by the time I had finished a really excellent breakfast, I had decided for the dramatic profession; there were agents I knew who arranged these matters, and these agents I determined to seek out and impress.

My first business was to cash a cheque and then

find a room. I couldn't stay in this hotel as a married lady whose husband had brought her at seven o'clock on a winter's morning and deserted her before the day was five hours older. George had settled the bill, an act of generosity at which, now, I rather wondered. Luckily I had a few shillings in my pocket with which to pay the necessary tips. That done, I put on my hat and set out without further delay for the bank on which Sir Thomas Lothmere, my recent benefactor, had drawn his cheque. It was pretty close by, in Piccadilly, and I walked.

The presentation of that cheque was really, I think, one of the most trying moments of my life. The cashier, a vulgar bourgeois man, looked me over with the most insulting deliberation, and I was made to feel at once that he supposed I had come by the cheque in no respectable fashion. I think old Sir Thomas was fairly good and proper; and even if, in former days, he had had occasion to make money presents to young ladies, I don't suppose he was fool enough to do it by cheque; so, perhaps, the worthy cashier had never before been called upon to hand over a sum of money to a very pretty girl in a smart hat, who presented a cheque signed by a widely respectable and elderly scientist. At last I got it; three crisp fivers and ten bright jingling sovereigns; and feeling much happier and on a sounder footing with the world, I set out on quest number two – lodgings.

Theatrical folk, one of whom I now proposed to be, inhabited principally, I had heard, strange and unknown lands across the water, called

Kennington and Camberwell and Brixton. I had never been on the Surrey side of the Thames in my life, and had no intention of going there now. So possibly very extravagantly, I determined to set myself up in the West End. My little costumiere. Eloise's friend, who had so kindly given me credit, lived close by in Jermyn Street, and it occurred to me that I might get a room over her shop.

Madame Karl lived in an old fashioned house in Jermyn Street. On the ground floor was her shop, a tiny *magasin de robes*, and the rest of the house was used for her own living rooms, and one or two sets of apartments, generally let out to bachelors. I found her in the shop, bowing out a plump lady of important mien.

She was genuinely glad to see me, and laughingly enquired how I managed to get my bill settled so soon. I made belief a few kisses had been all the price paid but I could see she thought I lied. With a laugh she pinched my cheek. 'Well, I wish all my customers were pretty girls,' she said. 'Then I should get my accounts settled more regularly. The lady that just went out owes me over a thousand pounds and on top of that she's just left an order to execute which I shall have to set aside all other work, and spend goodness knows how much on material. Yet I dare not offend her for she is the Countess of Alminster, and brings many American ladies here – who do pay. But it is a heavy commission,' and the little woman sighed and shrugged her shoulders.

Madame Karl was not exactly a beauty but she

had a figure that sets off to its best advantage by her perfect gowns and set many a man coveting the charms within. And the charms were worth having, as I discovered the first night I slept in the Jermyn Street House. She must have been thirty-eight or nine, but her flesh was firm and white and unwrinkled. I helped to rub her down with a soft towel before bed, and when I noticed how she wriggled under my fingers, I knew there was still a volcano of love in that pretty little body.

Our pact was soon sealed. I was to have one of the rooms upstairs, and Madame was very understanding about my paying rent at present. 'That can begin when you get an engagement,' she said.

In the meantime I was to make myself generally useful to her, and I soon gathered that many ways of making useful existed in that establishment.

'I let my chambers very easily to gentlemen,' she told me. 'It is so convenient, you know, should a lady call, for there to be a dressmaker's establishment on the ground floor; one may suspect a lady who enters a house let in gentlemen's apartments in Jermyn Street, but who shall question the right of a lady, married or single, to visit her dressmaker.'

So it came to pass that I was to be a sort of generally discreet chaperone. Madame used to give her lady clients tea in the upstairs sitting room. When the lady showed signs of being at all timid, I used to be present at the beginning of the tea, and then be suddenly called away, what time the gentleman accomplished his desire. More than a dozen times my errand did not take me further than the keyhole, and from that point of vantage I witnessed some quite amusing performances. I must say that some of Madame's aristocratic lady clients made no bones about haggling over the price of their bodies, just as if they had been ordinary women of the street.

Certainly the profits of the establishment appeared to be considerable; and one day, after a particularly good lunch, Madame Karl surprised me with her tale of the business done for the day.

'You remember the pretty little girl in the blue costume who came in here this morning,' she said, 'the one I left upstairs with you?'

I remembered perfectly well.

'She is Lord Wetlon's daughter. They are not at all well off, but naturally she loves pretty clothes. Well, you recollect the dark little gentleman who came in afterwards, whom you left up there with her. He is Christopher Echsstein, the broker. What she did for it, I don't know, but he ordered two hundred and fifty pounds worth of dresses for her, and, what is more, he gave me a cheque in advance. He's a true businessman, he wanted the discount.'

Madame had four assistants, all pretty girls, and each one of them hot as they make them. She didn't pay them much, but I reckon they had nothing to complain of about the little extra bits they made out of the husbands of some of her customers.

Of course, I attracted the attention, to say nothing of the lustful glances, of more than one of

Madame's trouser clad customers. Little Blanche was not the sort of beauty to go many days through her career without causing some masculine head to turn, or some masculine sexual members to press against the confining trousers in dumb protest. But the fools dared no more than a passing glance for I think they feared offending Madame Karl. Sometimes I was glad of their reticence, yet often again I so boiled over with desire to be made love to that I could have boxed the ears of several nice young men, who when left alone with me, looked their desire, but made no attempt to express it in more forceful, to say nothing of more pleasant, form. I honestly believe they thought me a virgin, I had looked so young, for I was not yet quite out of short frocks. That is to say, I wore a long gown and put up my hair in the evening, but the day time usually found my red-brown tresses gathered into a loose knot at the back of my neck and my ankles delightfully displayed by a short skirt which only journeyed three parts of the way down my calves. In fact, I was still a flapper.

'A little duck' I certainly looked, especially when I sat down and showed my pretty, rounded calves well up to the knee.

But, as I was saying, I occasionally felt almost uncontrollable pangs of naughtiness, and I am afraid that the fore-finger of my right hand was sometimes put to most improper uses – how I wished it had been a masculine digit! Once when Madame Karl and I were unusually confident (we were sitting over our tea and cigarettes and the fire), I let drop a hint of this. She was asking me about my seduction, and I told her that, although it was not all roses at the time, I would willingly have another try at fornication to relieve my lascivious feelings.

'And so you shall my dear girl,' she said, coming over to me and kissing me lovingly. 'Why nearly all the men who come here have begged of me to approach you on the subject, but I didn't like to.'

And so it was arranged, I was to go wrong with Lord X—.

'A Lord, Tut! tut!' this from Gladys.

'Oh, I've worked through pretty well and all the grades of the peerage in my time,' I answered, 'once I had a Viscount and a Duke in the same day.'

'And that reminds me of a story,' says Gladys. 'It concerns itself, does this little yarn, with a parson's wife, who by no means got all the pleasure she wanted out of her husband, the anaemic incumbent of a swagger West End parish. And it seems that it came to pass that one fine day Lord "So and So" visited her in the absence of her husband. Hearing someone coming she bade the Lord conceal himself on the top of the ancient four poster. He did so; but it was not her husband, only Sir C—, who had likewise went under the bed like a rabbit. This time it was her husband, come home randy for once in a way (he had been taking a girl's class) and he wanted it, too; and had it. At the conclusion, he remarked to his better-half, "Ah Mary, I sometimes think you have not always been as good a woman as you should

15

have been, but trust in the Lord above, He will look after you – .'

'Oh, will he?' came a voice from above the canopy. 'Then what about that bugger of a baronet underneath?'

It was arranged very artistically. I was not going to have it given away that I was a previously consenting party to the affair. Madame Karl, in the course of a casual conversation with Lord X, mentioned me: he declared his desire; she suggested he should go up to my bedroom, enter as if he had made a mistake (she told him that I would be undressing at the time), and it rested on his own initiative to complete the job.

I *was* undressing, that is to say I was pretty well in Eve's costume. Madame had warned me by speaking tube when he was nearly at the door, and when he entered he found me all stark naked but my chemise, and that fallen to my feet. Of course I uttered the time-honoured scream, covered my face with one hand and my mons veneris with the other, ran hither and thither about the room as if seeking cover and murmured, 'Oh go away; please!'

But he didn't go; he rushed at me, pulled one hand from my face and kissed me on the lips; pulled the other hand from my cunt and felt it, in fact, in about one minute he had got me down on the bed and his prick was well into me, not one single word did he say till I could feel him coming and the first part of the entertainment was over. As I lay back on the bed, panting, while he rather shamefacedly put back his penis into his trousers, I managed to gasp out: 'Well! What a funny way to make love to a girl! Don't you ever say anything?'

He laughed, 'I'm glad you're not furious,' he said, 'but to tell the truth I was awfully nervous.'

'Nervous?' He need not have been, for I don't mind betting I wanted it even more than he that blessed afternoon. 'Nervous!' How many a beautiful chance of exquisite sexual intercourse had been wasted by this wretched nervousness on the part of Mankind. I can call to mind the tale concerning a nervous person who asked another young man how he made small talk at parties, declaring himself always dumb on these occasions. 'Oh, I don't worry much about frills in my conversation,' was the answer, 'I just get the girl in a quiet corner, squeeze her hand and ask her if she likes fucking.'

'But my dear chap,' was the answer, 'what an awful thing to say; I should think you would get yourself badly disliked sometimes and get thrown out of the houses.'

'Well,' admitted the candid one, 'I do get disliked sometimes and I have been thrown out of houses, but I get a hell of a lot of fucking.'

MORAL – Oh – Mankind, remember that the woman is as often as not, as keen for it as you are – and don't be NERVOUS.

After that we got on splendidly. He undressed, was soon stiff and in again, and we had a long, glorious, slow grind, exquisite pleasure the whole time, and always that delightful feeling that there was much more ahead, not just a few more strokes and the business completed. Twice was all I would allow him, though he wanted more. I made him sponge me all over with hot scented water, rub me down till I glowed deliciously, and dress me. He was no novice at the game, and the teasing little kisses with which he would accompany all the business of drawing on my stockings, fastening my drawers, getting me into my corsets, etc., nearly made me fall again. When dressed at last, we went downstairs. I just found time to whisper to Madame Karl that it was satisfactorily done, and we got a cab and went off to have tea at Claridge's room among all the ambassadors.

Madame Karl seemed thoroughly pleased when I got back home. She was all over me, and gave me a hat lately arrived from Paris which I had coveted muchly. And as my lordling friend had bought me a diamond brooch at Streeter's, I did fairly well.

The secret of what I had done did not remain secret – I don't know how it got to the ears of the girls, but after dinner, when we were all together that evening, one of them got me alone in a corner of the drawing room and whispered. 'So you've been with Lord X—, this afternoon?' My blush was sufficient answer.

'Come out with me this evening,' she whispered, tickling my hand, 'I can promise you a lot of fun.'

Her tone, and the gesture with which she accompanied her invitation, gave me full well to understand that something naughty was in the wind. 'Must I ask Madame Karl's permission?' I asked.

'Of course.'

'My dear little Nemmy,' said Madame Karl, when I told her, 'of course you can go, but I warn you that this will be something quite out of the common. Nelly knows more than a bit.'

Now you mustn't run away with the idea that Madame Karl kept a bad house in the sense that her assistants were tarts and nothing else. As far as they were concerned, there was precious little wickedness performed on the premises; but Madame gave them a free hand on their off evenings; just as all the swagger dressmaker's establishments in London and Paris do.

'They all have their latch keys at Gay's, and at Madame Marie's, too,' says Gladys, 'I was at the latter for a bit myself and I know.'

Nelly was the youngest of Madame Karl's assistants, and only just promoted to the dignity of long skirts. She was a pretty blonde, very well favoured by nature, with a deliciously plump arm and shoulder, and very well developed breasts. Her legs were perfect; she was one of those few girls who could stand upright in an ordinary position, close her legs and keep a threepenny bit between her thighs. She was proud of this and often used to show us the trick.

She was delighted when I said I could come, and insisted on lending me a dress.

'Your own evening frock is delightful, my dear,' she explained, 'but it isn't quite what we want for this evening.'

She put me into a three-quarter length gown, extremely décolleté, but filled in about the shoulders with lace (which as a matter of fact, rather added to the suggestiveness of the confection). It was so low at the back that I had to wear a corset which was little more than a band around the waist, and my nipples almost escaped in front. She, too, put on a three-quarter dress, I began to see that this looked like a flapper party.

To cut a long story short, Nelly took me to a house in Cadogan Gardens, a swagger enough place to look at, and explained that it was kept by a woman of good family who added to her own rather diminished income by running it as a meeting place for men and girls. 'She's quite the best and nicest procuress in London,' Nelly explained, 'She's delightful to all the girls who go there, and you can be perfectly certain of your money.'

That there was money in the air, had never occurred to me when I accepted Nelly's invitation, but I didn't shrink on that account, I could do with a little of the root of all evil just then. Then Nelly told me that the parties varied. On one evening, for instance, our hostess would collect a few married women who were prepared to go astray from their titular lords and masters; sometimes quite young married women, and sometimes ladies who had attained the prime of life without losing their good looks – (these were for men who desired a lot of experience from their bedfellows) – and sometimes young girls.

'That'll be us, this evening,' I said.

I gathered from Nelly also that our hostess was prepared to find anything. She organized coster girl parties, bringing up pretty little East-Enders; and even parties at which very depraved young men could exercise their desire on quite elderly women. 'These parties,' said Nelly, 'are the most paying of all, for she gets money from both sides, since the old women are under the impression that she has to pay the young men – oh, she's very very clever.'

We were taken to Mrs Cowper in a large room which was a cross between a very elaborate boudoir and a hot house. That is to say, it was lighted by skylights like a studio, carpeted with some soft material into which one's feet sank almost to the ankles – I found out later that a thin mattress lay underneath the carpet – and was full of flowers and ferns of every kind. From the roof of an alcove depended a vine covered with luscious grapes. A table bearing a glittering tea equipment stood in one corner, various small tables bore wine and spirit decanters. We were ushered in and Mrs Cowper noticed me at once. 'Good Heavens, Nelly,' she cried, 'I had no idea you'd brought a stranger; whatever must she think of me, my dear?'

I could not do anything but blush, and Mrs Cowper continued: 'After all, I dare say Nelly has told you we're not very proper here,' and she laid her arms on my shoulders, kissing my lovingly on the lips.

Mrs Cowper was I suppose about thirty-five, and uncommonly beautiful. Her figure was perfection, and the dress she wore showed off all its delights. The dress was carried out in a design of ferns. Ferns, quite small at the waist, but gathering size as they fell lower, made the skirt; the bodice was one large bunch of ferns, out of which grew her ivory neck and shoulders; she had ferns in her hair, and two little pearl diamond ferns for earrings.

I sat by her side sipping a liqueur while Nelly briefly told her who and what I was.

'You'll do for me very nicely, dear girl,' she said, 'I think you will just suit a man I've got coming this evening; let me see, are you a virgin?'

I had half framed the word yes, when she suddenly ran her hand up my clothes, and felt my trembling little cunt – 'Oh no, you're not,' she said, with a laugh, 'and you must not pretend to be. I never deceive my patrons *here*.'

'I've only been wrong with two men,' I said, pouting.

'Well, your third will be young Mr Robinson, of the Stock Exchange. I shall charge him ten pounds for you and give you five of it; whatever you get out of him on the top of that is of course your own affair. Here is the fiver,' she handed me a note.

'And me?' said Nelly.

'A Mr Reichardt, likewise of the Stock Exchange, a friend of his, they will be here in a moment.'

But before those worthies arrived, a number of other girls were shown in. Some arrived singly, but more often they came in twos or threes. I reckon there were about fifteen present before a single trousered animal put in an appearance. They were pretty and, beautiful though I knew myself to be, I felt I had plenty of rivals on this occasion. Some were very young – wicked as I was I could help not feeling it rather a shame when I saw girls who could not have been more than sixteen – and I don't suppose one there was more than twenty-one. All were pretty, often very extravagantly dressed, and I have never since, despite all the varied experience of my life seen such a delightful assemblage of dainty shoulders, plump little girlish arms, well moulded calfs, generally displayed to the knee, and slim attractive little waists.

About a dozen men arrived, and we had music – and a good many drinks. Everything was very decorous; Nelly told me that no impropriety went on *coram populo*, and I flirted in an amiable manner with my Mr Robinson. An occasional touch of his hand gave me naughty shivers, to say nothing of the frequent discreet comminglings of his trousers with my stockings, and I had begun to wonder when there was going to be any serious play, when Nelly took me aside.

'Mrs Cowper wants me to ask you a favour, Blanche dear,' she said, 'It seems there are not quite enough men to go around.

'*Shocking mismanagement – !' interrupts Gladys.*

'And she doesn't want any of the girls left over.'

'*Prudent woman,' the irrepressible typewriter again.*

'Wherefore she wants to know whether you and

23

I will go with the same man – it's that old gentleman over there – (pointing to a lean and lanky old sportsman who was doing prodigies with the spirit decanters in a secluded corner, feasting his eyes on the girls at intervals) – 'it'll be another fiver each,' she concluded.

I was rather glad. I liked Nelly, and I hadn't much modesty even then. I felt that I should be much less nervous, with her to aid, than alone, so the bargain was struck. Mrs Cowper, first giving me the extra fiver – she was extremely business-like – sidled us up to our fare; we went with him into another room and had a little stand up supper against a buffet. Then Mrs Cowper led the conversation round to art, told our friend that we were art students, said that we were dying to see the Correggio in the pink boudoir, and left him to take us there – it was so tactful and nice.

Our old friend got us into the boudoir in due course, and all the time I was wondering where I had seen his face before. Then I tumbled to the fact that his beard and moustache were false – (I noted that while he was kissing me) – and got it. He was the senior classical master at Rocton, my father's school. At first, came terror that he was likely to recognise me, but I soon saw that he was quite oblivious to my identity – in fact I had changed a bit since he could have seen me last. Then it occurred to me to frighten him – not that any idea of blackmail had ever crossed my mind – no.

He fucked Nelly first – to be blunt; not, I trust, because he didn't think me the nicest, but because it appeared that he had had Nelly before, and was less nervous. There wasn't much art about it at all. I just sat on the edge of the couch and smoked a cigarette while he stripped her naked, kissed her in many places and generally messed her about, till he finally produced a giant weapon, and shoved it up her. The consummation was short. Nelly seemed frantically randy, wriggled her arse like a tortured soul, and soon had him spending into her for all he was worth.

By that time I, naturally, was naughty too, but I had to wait a bit; that greedy Nelly had got too much, and we had to aid our friend with much manipulation of his person, tickling his balls, stroking of his little stomach, etc., before he had me on the sofa with his lance in me – the rest was easy, and I kept in till the moment I could feel him swelling with rapidly arriving semen, when I said, very quietly. 'Whatever would Michael Hunt say if he saw you doing this?'

The man gave one convulsive wriggle, shot about a gallon of fluid into me, then rolled off, pale to the hair roots – 'What do you know about Michael Hunt?' he asked.

'Only that you're his senior master at Rocton. I know you very well by sight, even if you have a false beard and moustache on. I do hope you've enjoyed this better than to teach at the boys school.'

Now anyone but a fool would have seen the fun of the thing and laughed with us. Nelly told me afterwards he must have known that Mrs Cowper's was a safe enough place, and felt no

25

fear of blackmail – but that silly old thing wacked up fifty pounds for us two to divide, so that we should be mum. I don't say that he didn't have a bit more fun for his money – but fifty is a lot, and I daresay he had paid Mrs Cowper quite a tidy sum already.

Still, this is a little bit by the way, and I must get back to that first day of mine at Madame Karl's.

She took me out to dinner on the first evening of my stay, we went to a small but extremely smart restaurant in the very heart of innermost St James's. Madame knew most of them – the men and women – by sight, and told me their names. She might have been reciting Debrett by the page. When I noted the price of the food, and especially the wine, I was astounded. Madame must assuredly be very rich to afford this.

We did ourselves well, and drank only the oldest vintages, but when the bill was brought she simply signed it on the back and gave the waiter half a crown. A light began to dawn upon me.

'It's like reverting to the old system of barter, isn't it?' said madame with a laugh. 'I dress the manager's wife at a reduction and the manager feeds me. I don't suppose his directors know anything about it.'

As soon as we had appeared to have settled our bill several men whom madame knew crossed the room to speak to us; but she got rid of them all, suggesting to me that we should go to a music hall.

We had a box at the music hall without paying for it. 'More barter,' said madame. 'That silly little man's wife would never have reached her present position on the stage without the aid of my frocks.'

I began to think that Madame Karl was an exceeding power in the land, and also to doubt whether there wasn't something in the dress-making business after all. I determined to make myself useful to her. I think I must have created somewhat of a sensation in that hall, for upon the door of our box beat an endless tattoo, and from the stalls necks were craned upwards, and a variety of male humanity studied me through opera glasses. It must have been me, for Madame Karl sat back in the shadow.

I did not enjoy the performance; few women figured among the turns; it was a carnival of comedians and a hymn of praise to vulgarity. The audience roared at the antics of the various little red-nosed men who occupied the stage, but the humours of the enterprising lodger, the confiding landlady, and their illicit amours, and the ever recurring Bacchanal drink chant palled most terribly, and I was intensely relieved when madame recognized a friend and signalled to him to come and see us.

Mr Runthaler was a gentleman of a comfortable person, an expensive fur coat and a deal of jewellery. Madame had forewarned me that he had a great deal of interest in matters theatrical, and I was very nice to him; he was in return very nice to me, in fact, rather too nice, for the semi-publicity of a box at a music hall. I found an early opportunity of broaching the subject of the stage. 'Well, little girl,' he answered, 'if you want to be an actress, take my advice and don't go to the agents; they'll never get you a London engagement, and I presume you don't want to spend your life tramping the provinces in a second rate musical comedy company. If you want to play at a West End Theatre, you must get at the managers personally, and for a girl like you I don't think it'll be very hard. If you like, I'll give you an introduction to my friend Lewis, of the Duke's Theatre, he'll see any girl I send. I should advise you to try and catch him tonight; besides, that frock suits you.'

He left us directly, after pencilling a few words of introduction on his card, and soon afterwards I persuaded Madame to come with me to the Duke's Theatre.

The hall porter took the card and handed it to a young gentleman in faultless evening dress, who stood in the hall. The latter examined us at some length, enquired which was Miss La Mare, and then said that Mr Lewis was not at present in the theatre, but that if I went round to his flat in the next street he might possibly see me. He wrote something on the card in a language which I took to be Yiddish, and handed it back to me. Word came down that Mr Lewis would see me at once, and, closely followed by Madame Karl, I went up. We were shown into a large apartment extravagantly decorated in the Japanese manner, and so draped about the walls and ceilings with curtains that it had the appearance of a tent. The chief furniture of the place was an enormous divan extending nearly the whole length of the room; a few tables, mostly covered with bottles and glass of rare and antique design, were arranged in deliberate disorder; two large pictures represented classical and, incidentally, indelicate events; and there were a couple of capacious easy chairs; an upright grand piano, and that was all. In the middle of the divan, arrayed in a smoking suit and one that rivalled the storied coat of his ancestor Jacob, squatted, pasha fashion, Mr Lewis.

He was a little round man, with a straight line of curling black hair across his lip, and a head that was entirely bald. As he sat there he looked like a Hebraic Humpty Dumpty. He made no attempt to rise, but welcomed us with a nod and an expression of annoyance, obviously caused by the presence of my companion.

'You are Miss La Mare, I presume,' he said glancing from the card in his hand to me. 'Blanche La Mare – it should look well on a bill. And you want to be an actress. Well, what can you do, Miss La Mare?'

I answered that I could sing and he motioned me to the piano.

'Sing something light,' he said.

I selected a song out of Mirelda which I remembered. After the first verse he stopped me.

'Very nice, very nice indeed,' he said. 'And now, Miss La Mare, I cannot talk business before a third person; would your friend mind leaving us for a while?' Madame made a gesture of dissent, but though I was pretty sure what was coming, I had thought I'd better see it out, so I asked her to go.

When we were alone, Mr Lewis left his divan and came towards me. 'Well, you're a very pretty little lady,' he said. 'I think you may suit me, just take your coat off, and let's see your shoulders. Ah, very nice too,' and he patted my neck affectionately. 'And what pretty lips, may I?' Without waiting for an answer, he kissed me. I made no resistance. I was quite prepared to pay this sort of tribute.

'Very nice,' he said again, smacking his fat lips, 'so far most satisfactory, and now let's see what sort of legs you have got.'

Madame had told me that the usual way adopted by a burlesque manager for making sure of the suitability of a girl's legs was for the girl to draw her legs tight round the members in question, and this I did.

'Ah, yes, but I'm afraid I can hardly tell by that, dear little lady,' he chuckled, 'you know my patrons are very particular about legs. Don't be shy now, pull your clothes up and let me see what they really are like.'

I blushed, for I felt ashamed, but I did it. I lifted my clothes well above my knees, and as I was wearing rather short drawers, the perfect contour of my lower leg and a good deal of the upper part was plainly visible.

He asked me to stretch them apart, and I

obeyed, blushing the more. He came quite close and leered at my limbs through his glasses.

'I think you'll do, my little dear,' he said. 'I'll go and get a contract form. You will be undressed when I get back, won't you?'

'I don't know what you mean.'

'Yes, you do, my dear, you understand me perfectly. If you had been a modest girl you wouldn't have shown me your legs. I like you and I should like to engage you, but before I sign the contract I'm going to enjoy you; what's there to make a fuss about in that?'

It was a bit too cold-blooded, and I could not stand it – 'Well, you've made a mistake this time,' I said, 'I may not be a modest girl, as you put it, but there are limits. So Good-bye.'

He did not seem angry; 'Ah, well, he said. 'you're a little fool, engagements with me are good and comfortable and profitable. I like you because you're more than ordinarily pretty, but I'm not going to relax my rule. I always have my chorus girls, once at least, and I can't begin making exceptions now. Perhaps one of these days you'll think it over and come back to me again.'

'No, that I will never, you dirty old mean beast,' I answered, moving towards the door.

He laughed again; 'Don't go for a minute,' he said, 'I promise you I won't try to force you, but I should like to argue with you. Now, you're not a virgin, I'm certain of that; you do yourself no harm by just lying down on the sofa and letting me have you, and you'll get an engagement. I shall not want to have you anymore.' Then, before I realised what he was up to, he had slipped his hand between his legs, flicked open his fly and was holding out an erect penis for my inspection. With his other hand he grabbed my shoulder and slipped his foot between my legs, tripped me up.

I fell heavily, and if it had not been for the softness of the carpet I think I should have hurt myself. In a moment the little beast was on top of me, holding my shoulders down with his two hands while he tried to force his knee between my legs. I had fallen with one leg a little apart from the other, and he succeeded in that part of his fell purpose. He scraped my dress up somehow, and in fact got as far as banging the end of his panting member against my stomach – but that was all. I had no intention of letting the brute conquer me, and at the moment he thought victory secure, and took one of his hands from my shoulders to help guide his weapon to its grave. I let him have it with my right hand full on the end of his nose. The blow gave him fair hark from the tomb, as my young friend Charley Lothmere would have phrased it in his quaint Pink'un English, and the blood gushed from the damaged proboscis. It only made him think better of his attempt, and he got up, swearing under his breath, bursting into a roar of laughter.

Oddly enough, as soon as I found myself outside, I felt as randy as hell, and somewhat repented my action.

When I was back at Jermyn Street I told Madame what had happened.

She did not exactly applaud my action, 'Well, you know dear, you're not a virgin,' she said, 'and I must say that I don't think it would have done much harm.'

'The harm was in your being a virgin for damned near a whole volume of this immortal work,' breaks in the irrepressible Gladys, 'and I'd have let the old swine fuck me if he was going to give me an engagement.'

'I would have, perhaps, if he hadn't tried to force me,' I answered.

'Force you!' says Gladys, with a tinge of scorn in her voice, 'why I'm damned if I don't think it's half the pleasure. Listen – would you like to hear what happened to me?'

THE STORY OF GLADYS

It was during my first typewriter's job in London. I was not a virgin, but I was at that time what I should call quite a moral girl, that is to say I stuck to one man. I resisted the daily efforts of my business employer, and used to hurry home in the evenings to my Bloomsbury lodging. Twice a week I met my lover who took me to dinner, and subsequently to a furnished room in one of the good old flea ravaged hotels in the Euston Road. It was there, after my young man, who knew a bit, had plentifully peppered the bed with good old Keating, we enjoyed ourselves to to the top of love's young delight. We could not afford a more frequent connection, for Albert lived with his family and drew but three pounds a week for his lusts and living, while the boarding house inhabited by myself drew a strict line at young men visitors.

Well on one occasion, a dark and dreary winter's evening, just after a happy time with my young man, who at the time I sincerely loved, I was making my way home through foggy bleared streets, when my way was blocked by a tall figure that loomed up through the darkness and grasped me by the arm. 'Forgive me for stopping you,' he said, 'but there is a woman hard by in sore distress, and we cannot find another of her sex to be with her. Will you come?' His voice seemed so naturally affected that I could not find it in my heart to say nay, and I went.

The man treated me with the greatest consideration and deference, apologising for the queer route our journey took us. At last we came to a tall, ugly house. After two flights of creaking stairs, a door opened to admit us into a seemingly very comfortable flat. Another man had opened the door, but he was silent as I and my companion passed him. I began to feel a little nervous, but the sound of a woman's voice calling in tones which seemed shaking with pain, 'Have you got her, John?' – reassured me.

I followed my guide, whom I now saw, in the light of the flat, to be a powerfully built, strong faced, ugly man with penetrating eyes, into a bedroom. Between the sheets lay a woman, whom at first glance I recognised as a singularly beautiful creature. She was quite small and slight, a little thin in the neck perhaps, and pinched great eyes. In those great eyes which seemed to dominate the room, lay her chief cute charm. She did not look particularly ill, and I was surprised to note that she appeared to be quite naked, for the arm which lay on the coverlet was bare, and there was no sign of a garment about her neck and shoulders. Her fingers were covered with rings; it was obviously no poor woman who needed my assistance. In fact I summed her up at once as a well to do prostitute.

I was advancing towards the bed about to speak to her, when I felt my waist surrounded by the man's arms. At the same moment, I noticed a smile on the face on the woman. As I tried to struggle from his embrace it struck me that I was trapped, and the woman's words which immediately followed only too well confirmed my suspicion. 'You've collared a pretty one, John,' she purred in a mocking tone. As my glance ran round the room, I saw that now the third man was present, sitting in a chair by the door, smoking a cigar.

'What does this mean?' I cried, in a choking voice.

For answer the big man gripped me again and kissed me violently.

'I implore you, what does it mean?' I said to the woman.

'Only that you must be a good girl and do what you're asked,' she responded with an irritating smile, and at the same time the big man forced me back against the bed.

'Oh, tell me what you do want; is it money?' I begged, the tears welling into my eyes.

'No, you little fool,' the man answered savagely, 'we want to fuck you!' and he let me go, then continued, 'undress yourself quickly – or else we'll make you.'

I screamed at the top of my voice, but was answered by a general laugh. Then I swung round towards the woman and raised my hand, threatening her. In a second I found my legs twitched from under me and I was sprawled upon the floor. One man held my knees down and the other my elbows.

As I lay there quite helpless, the woman slipped from her bed, a beautiful little devil she was too, in her nakedness, superbly well formed, though on the small scale, with a perfect skin. She pressed my waist down with her two hands and looked into my eyes. 'Will you be undressed quietly, and let these men do what they like?' she cooed.

I made no answer.

Then they tied me down, by my ankles and wrists, to the legs of the bed on one side, and to a couple of rings which were also used for some sort of gymnastic appliance, on the other. My legs were stretched wide apart.

Now perhaps it may seem rather exciting, but at that time, you must remember, I was only eighteen, deeply in love, and had been wrong with two men only.

I was mad with rage. They made no further attempts to cajole me, in fact, had I known as much as I do now, I should have seen that the very fact of forcing me was three parts of the pleasure to these sinister people.

The woman took a razor from the toilet table. I shut my eyes, fearing some horrible outrage, but she only used it to rip my dress and petticoats to my waist. The halves of my costume she turned over, laying bare my drawers and a good deal of the naked lower part of my stomach, for I wore no corsets.

She laid her hand on my little mount of Venus, and fingered it affectionately, though she did not succeed in producing the least little thrill in me. I was far too angry. But the sight seemed to please the men, for, with a simultaneous action they each produced a large and erect prick and balls from their trousers and stood over me.

The woman completed my undressing, ripping off everything completely and destroying my clothes. When I was left naked on the damned floor, there was some affair of tossing up between the men as to which one should get a nice hot fuck out of me. The big one won, and promptly disembarrassed himself out of his clothes. I was perfectly helpless, and compelled to lie there awaiting the ravishing of this brute, but he hesitated.

'I don't think I want the girl tied down like a log,' he said, 'let her go and I will try to manage it.'

Well, they did let me go, the woman had no

hand in this. I fancy she was rather nervous. She perched herself crosswise on the bed, lit a cigarette and waited. I still lay there when I was freed, but found myself jerked up to my feet, and then the big man grappled with me. I just managed to get my teeth well into his shoulder, and with a right hand to grip him savagely by the balls, and I felt a heavy blow behind the ear and remembered no more.

I came to my senses to find a man on top of me, his prick deep into me, and the girl bathing my temples with brandy. I felt far too ill then to struggle more as the man finished without extracting the tiniest drop of reciprocal juice from me.

My ravisher lay heavily upon me, seemingly disinclined to remove himself from so pleasant a position, and the thing within me stayed stiff and unyielding, but the other man jerked my ravisher's shoulders up.

'Easy now, don't flatten the girl,' he said, then I felt the weight of the man's stomach relax, and his mighty cock slip out of my cunt. It was odd, but the moment his penis slid from me I experienced a thrill of pleasure; not pleasure that the thing had been removed, but real sensual joy, then I burst into tears.

They treated me kindly, lifted me gently on to the bed, and smoothed my limbs with their hands. The woman brought me warm water and bathed my thighs. Why I had bled I can't think; for, as you know, Blanche dear, I wasn't a virgin at that time, far from it. I suppose it must have been my wriggling, and the quite exceptional size of the man's member. But they certainly thought I was a virgin.

'Poor little thing,' said the woman cooingly, 'You'll soon get to love it and you will thank us for initiating you in the art of love.'

I did not speak a word, but lay immobile wondering what would happen to me next. The other man's prick was stiff as a ramrod, and I felt certain I was not going to leave that room till he had gratified himself.

Then the woman slipped down on the bed by my side, and folded me in her arms. The delicate softness of her reconciled me to my position. Gently I returned her caress and in another moment our lips met in a loving kiss. She was very, very pretty; her lips were soft, her breath fragrant, and she followed the kiss by a delicate fondling of my clitoris. My position on the bed enabled me to see a mirror on the other side of the room, and the sight of our soft, white bodies thus folded together entranced me. I wriggled in her arms, darted my tongue between her teeth, and coveted that wandering finger of hers. In a flash I realised that for the first time in my life I was consumed with physical desire for the body of another being of my own sex. I abandoned myself entirely to her kisses.

Glady's words inflamed me. Ever since I had had the pretty girl as an amanuensis, I had known she was delightful to look at, and more than once I had caught myself regarding her with a feeling

39

which had certainly something more than mere friendship and admiration in it. At last I had come to the conclusion that I wanted her, but I dared make no attempt till she herself confessed through her story that she had before been enjoyed by a woman.

I made the getting of a drink a pretext to leave my chair, I poured out stiff glasses of whisky and soda for both of us, and in handing Gladys hers, allowed my hand to stray over her soft shoulder, we were working, as usual, at night, and Gladys still wore her theatre gown, an extremely décolleté confection, that is to say she retained its bodice, but the skirt she had taken off, and sat in her petticoat, a pretty silk thing of dark red colour which allowed her legs to be visible almost to the knee; her lace silk stockings were so very open-worked that the little threads seemed traced with a pen on her gleaming white flesh. She was very desirable to look at, and that must be my excuse.

'I don't marvel at the woman, Gladys,' I whispered in her little pink ear.

Then I kissed her just below the ear, and let my free hand wander over her neck down to where the bosom began to swell out of her corsage. She bent her head forward and bit my fingers softly.

We were both nervous, such an affair between us had never been mentioned, perhaps even thought of on her part, and for quite five minutes I remained kissing her cheek softly while she fondled my hand with her lips. Then, emboldened by the mad passion within me, I slipped to my knees, and ran my hand underneath her dress, up, up to her knees, and on, boldly on, to the bare flesh above her stockings, and at last to the opening between her drawers which gave me free ingress to her delicious front door of lust. Her legs were wide apart, and the lips of her vagina seemed red hot. I could feel her kisses covering my neck while my finger penetrated that sweet grotto.

Suddenly she jumped up. 'Blanche, darling,' she panted, 'come to the photograph studio.

The photograph studio in my house is a large room (only a few yards from the boudoir where I as a rule dictate this thrilling romance) which we are in the habit of using for taking naked pictures of each one of us.

I followed Gladys and closed the door behind us. In almost less time than it takes to write it, she had freed herself from the underclothes and lay naked, entrancing, voluptuous, on the great couch. All my nervousness was gone in an instant, and my undressing was almost as speedy.

Then I buried my head between her thighs.

I seemed to remain there for hours, although the dear girl told me afterwards that it could not have been more than ten minutes before she freed herself. I could not see her face, but her image was clear in my eyes, and each thrill of her thighs, that told me of enjoyment she extracted from my act, urged my tongue to more passionate embraces. At last she pushed my head from between her legs, my face was covered with love juice. She seized my head between her hands, I

41

had not till then known how strong she was, and kissed the spend from it.

'Now!' she cried, when the last kiss was ended, 'it is my turn!'

I lay back on the sofa, opening my legs to their widest extent, and she gently licked. Her tongue seemed like a javelin charged with the electricity of lust. It darted round my clitoris, softly swept the little space between that excrescence and my gaping cunt, and stabbed strongly into me. I seemed to experience nothing but one long, voluptuous spend. When at last she left me, I lay back exhausted.

We were too tired for more of that vigorous sensuality, but for an hour or more we sprawled on the couch in each other's arms, and our lips were seldom apart.

We got back to work on the immortal memoir very late next morning. Gladys said no word of our overnight frolic, simply giving me a type-written copy of the rest of her story, which you shall have directly. I had already sent down, by my maid, my notes of our little affair in the photograph boudoir.

Here is the rest of Gladys' tale.

The two men did not suffer me to stay long in the arms of the woman. I was forcibly removed and the second man stretched me on the rug. In three strokes he possessed me, but kept his place and worked hard until he came again. I was dripping with spend when at last he left me, but he was no sooner off, than my first ravisher took his place, fucked me heartily, and deluged my sore and tired vagina with more love juice.

I lay panting on the floor while he wiped his dripping cock on the long hair of the woman, rather a pretty little trick, I thought, and wondered what was likely to befall me next, when there came a ring at the bell. I was about to jump up, but was held down at once, you can imagine that I had very little strength of resistance, and had the mortification of seeing two more men, strangers to me of course, come into the room where I lay naked on the floor. One was a tall, splendidly made young fellow; the other an elderly man. Both were in evening dress. Both seemed to take my presence there rather as a matter of fact, and kissed the woman as if nothing unusual was in the wind. In fact I was rather neglected, for the young man began stroking the woman's legs and suddenly took on a fury of passion, flung up her chemise, stretched her on the bed, and was into her in a tick. It was a short and wanton fuck.

My turn however came next, and I fell to the lot of the old man, who did not even take the trouble to remove any of his clothes; but fucked me rather laboriously, though apparently with a great deal of satisfaction to himself. When at last he did spend, he announced the fact with some pride, and received the plaudits off the rest. As soon as he was off me the woman bent down and examined my thighs: 'It's true,' she cried, 'my congratulations, Sir Richard,' and she fell to licking the sticky stuff from my legs. 'It's not often I get a chance of tasting any of your spend,' she said, as some sort of explanation of her wanton act.

Then commenced an orgy. The young man mounted me; Sir Richard screwed himself into the woman, and I was scandalised to see, by means of the mirror, that the other two proceeded to get into the young man and Sir Richard '*per annus*' as the classics have it. The weight up on me was considerable, but, whether it was the performance going on in his back door, or whether he really was very much inflamed by my charms the young man fucked me beautifully, and, tired as I was, I enjoyed it. We three were finished long before Sir Richard's party, and the entertainment concluded with my squatting above the woman's mouth, so that she employed her tongue in my arse hole, while Sir Richard licked my cunt, what time I took the young man's prick in my mouth. It was somewhat of an elaborate piece.

'I should think it was indeed,' was my comment, when I had read this amazing confession.

'And that,' concluded Gladys, 'is the end of the story. I won't bore you with further details. There was only one other thing of interest about the affair.'

'And what was that?' I asked.

'They gave me ten pounds,' said Gladys, 'a sum of money which I could very well do with at the time.'

2

'I speak in English,' Madame Karl would frequently say, 'I write in English, now-a-days I even think a good deal in English, but breakfast in English I never have done, and I never will.'

Wherefore, when in response to a gently graduated series of knocks on my door I woke on the first morning of my stay at Jermyn Street, it was to find Christine the maid, bearing my *café complet* on a silver tray.

Madame, she informed me, would join me presently, then, as she drew aside the curtains, the crisp, clear winter's light ran into the room, and swept what was left of the dustman's sleep from my eyes.

I must say I like breakfasting in bed; the meal is a necessity at the best of it, not a luxury; wherefore it should be consumed with the least inconvenience and the most luxurious surroundings possible. I experienced a delightful feeling of ease that bright morning as I lay in my pretty bed and sipped the coffee. I had to get out of bed for a moment, and went to the window and looked down on the street below. I could see through an open space in the houses opposite to where Piccadilly roared in full flood, the sun glittering on the panels of the carriages and the cabs, bright and cheery and genial and good natured; so it all seemed. One could hardly be otherwise than good tempered on that perfect morning, and in that jolly room.

Presently Madame Karl slid into the room, a dream of a little woman in a sort of breakfast jacket which was more than principally openwork in its style. It was just nicely calculated to make an otherwise fired out man feel it incumbent on him to have a final fuck in the morning. Her little round pink breasts were glowing under the openwork, with the nipples showing quite plainly. The contour of her body and legs was more suggestive than if they had been seen quite naked. Of course she did not look absolutely fresh; but she was quite carefully prepared.

She sat on the edge of my bed, displaying twelve inches of pretty leg swathed in black silk stocking, and yawned. 'The morning sometimes brings regrets to a widow, my dear Blanche,' she sighed.

I kissed her lips, and I am quite sure that at that minute we both of us thought of other kisses presented by beings bearing a distinctive badge of sex between the thighs.

But about breakfast. Even at Lady Exwell's, where we were supposed to be very smart, the meal did not approach anything like geniality.

There the massive table used to be littered with a profusion of indigestible dishes, and the sideboard groaned beneath the weight of the cold viands. The woman came down shirted and collared and tailor-made gowned, and the talk turned inevitably to the slaughter of beasts. I have only one affectionate memory of the early morning habits of that house, and that was when a new footman, mistaking my bedroom for one of the gentlemen's, marched in with a tray bearing a decanter of brandy, a syphon, and a pint of champagne. Seeing his mistake, the worthy fellow would have fled, but I hailed him in no uncertain tones, and put away my small bottle like the best man in the house. I found out afterward that the midshipman had been monkeying with the boots in the passage, and put a pair of old Sir George's easy twelves outside my virgin portal. However, I kept up my habit of the morning bottle till I found out that the liveried idiot had been inventing gallantries on his part to Lady Exwell's maid, whereupon there was a suspicion of a scandal, and the morning pints had to be stopped. At Sir Thomas Lothmere's the breakfasts were of the same solemn and elephantine nature, aggravated by the preface of family prayers, read by the arch scamp, George Reynolds.

Breakfast undoubtedly is a meal that needs to be tackled in private and in bed. You may say what you will about rosy cheeked, healthy English girls who go on flower picking excursions in the garden on an empty stomach, and you may prate about the mushroom that you have plucked youself, tasting the best – a statement to which I unhesitatingly give the lie – but girls do not look their best at breakfast, and as it is their duty to conceal themselves during the hours when they do not please, let them break their fast in the seclusion of their chambers. Then think of the comfort of it; no horrid clamorous gong to wake one from delightful morning dreams, no enforced appearance at a fixed hour, to be mechanically pleasant to other people who are just as cross as you are yourself; but when you have decided that the right time has come, just a pressure of the bell, and in a few minutes your breakfast, and your letters, which you can read without the suspicion that your next door neighbour is looking over your shoulder.

We dressed leisurely, each admiring the pretty body of the other. It was strange how firm Madame Karl's skin was, how round her buttocks and her breasts, considering her age and very considerable experience of a gay life. Upon my word, she had nearly as good a figure as I, and at that time I really think that a looking glass seldom reflected more perfect charms than those supplied by Blanche's naked little body. I used to flatter myself, in fact, that if I failed to do any good on the stage, the career of a model in the altogether was always open to me. In fact, once during my stay with Madame, during a period of hard-up-ness and at that time when I was particularly anxious not to touch the dear little Madame for any money, I did put my pride in my pocket and have a round of the studios. After trying about five I found a man who wanted a model for the figure.

He was very blunt about it. I was consigned behind the screen, and came back naked to the world, to pose before a critical eye, now additionally armed with a pair of glasses. He decided I would do, and I got to work there and then as he had a picture on the stocks. I don't quite know where he intended to exhibit the picture; even the French salon, I should have thought, would have shied at it. It represented a pretty girl at her toilet. She was naked, all save her stockings, and she was taking the advice of an elderly man with her, as to which set of underclothes she should select. The flesh tints of the girl were gorgeously done, and the whole thing was full of suggestiveness. The man in the bedroom was fully dressed.

'Still, this is a little apart from the story, isn't it.' interrupted Gladys. 'I have been an artist's model myself, but it isn't one of the episodes in my life that I care to dwell on. Still an artist hadn't any of the negative attributes. He was not a mannikin with crinkly skin over him, but a big, bluff young man, fresh from Slade school, who used to make me pose for an hour or so, then fuck me on the sofa for another hour or so, and finally take me out to a remarkably fine lunch. It was a sweet thing, his penis, a good eight inches long, and perfectly shaped; and the best of it was he knew how to use it so as to give pleasure to the girl as well as to himself. How he could fuck!'

'Talking of penises,' I break in, 'what do you consider a really large one?'

'Ten inches, of course is Brobdignagian,' answers Gladys, 'but I must say that I have met a good many which measured quite eight on the foot rule. Still,

49

after all, the size of a man's weapon is only a matter of curiosity; it is a thing which pleases one to look at, but I don't think at all, the actual length or girth makes any difference to the enjoyment of the fornication. It's the way he uses it.'

I remember a negroe who once – but it's an awful story, and I'll spare you telling – still he had a thing on him which must have measured a good foot. George Reynolds, my seducer, though not a very big man, had a pretty plaything to flatter a girl with.

However, to get back once more to the tale . . .

A few days after my disappointing interview with Lewis, Madame told me she thought it quite time an excursion was made to the agents. To gain that end she first proposed to introduce me to a journalist friend of hers who had some little influence in theatrical circles.

Madame showed me the paper with which her friend was connected, a publication bound in an offensively light green colour, and labeled 'The Moon' in heavy black lettering. I knew the paper, it was one of Charley Lothmere's favourites. It contained weekly stories, under the heading of 'What the Man in the Moon Thinks' that suited Charley's taste exactly. They were very much up to date and frequently improper, wherefore it was with considerable surprise that I subsequently learned that they were all written by an elderly widowed lady, resident in Scotland.

We found the office of the 'Moon' at last in a small street running from the Strand, and Madame sent her card in.

The office boy took her card through an inner

door and we heard the sound of his voice, but none answering. Some minutes passed, but dead silence reigned in the room within. Then Madame, who was becoming impatient, signed to me to follow, and herself followed the boy through the door. We found ourselves in a large, comfortably furnished room that looked on to a small courtyard and was quite apart from the distracting noises of the outside world. In the centre of the room stood a square table of considerable size, bearing a large variety of newspapers, a whisky bottle, several syphons, and a half dozen glasses or so. In three armchairs in various corners of the room, sat three men all fast asleep. One of them was tall and fair, his face was clean shaven, and he was rather haggard, he was dressed a little elaborately, and wore a large button-hole in the lapel of his frockcoat. I should have guessed his age to be about twenty-six. A second was of medium size, and might have been any age. His hair fell in thick masses about the sides of his head, his moustache was twisted upwards with an assumption of ferocity, but in his sleep it was easy to see that he was really a very mild man. In the best armchair, and nearest the fire, sat a little man whom I took to at once. He was short, and of a well-rounded, comfortable figure, but it was in the extreme youthfulness of his appearance, that lay his charm. His hair was long, and fell in carefully disposed ringlets over his forehead into his blue eyes. His whole chubby countenance was wrapped in a seraphic smile, and in his left hand he still grasped a tumbler.

He was snoring somewhat and with each snore the smile broadened across his face; doubtless he was dreaming some happy boyish fancy, and his spirit was wandering in some pure noble land, far away from the worldly turmoil of the Strand.

'The long one is Mr Annesley,' said Madame, and advancing towards him she prodded him sharply in the ribs with her umbrella. He uncurled like a coiled spring that is suddenly released, and stood bolt upright, his hands instinctively seeking his hair to see if it was neatly brushed.

'My dear Madame Karl,' he ejaculated, 'a thousand pardons for the condition of the men in the Moon, but it is the day after publishing day, you see, and we are taking a well deserved rest. Will you come with me into the next room?'

I followed them rather reluctantly, for I was anxious to see what the little man was like when awake. We came into a comfortable little room wherein sat a young lady who was doing her hair before a glass, on the table before her lay several envelopes addressed to the editresses of ladies papers.

'This is Lilly,' said Mr Annesley, 'Lilly of the Valley,' we call her, because she toils not, etc., but it is not quite fair, because, though she does not toil, and probably, if you set her before a spinning wheel she'd think it was sort of a new bicycle, yet she spins the most excellent yarns to undesirable callers.'

'Oh, Mr Annesley,' said the girl, 'you do tell them,' and finishing the tying of her hair with a determined twist, she left the room. Almost immediately we heard the sound of a smart blow on flesh followed by a short boyish cry.

'That's nothing,' said Mr Annesley, 'that's only Lilly's way of telling the boy to go and stand outside while she sits in his chair. And now, Madame Karl, I am very much at your service, what can I do for you?'

'First of all,' said Madame, 'let me introduce you to Miss Blanche La Mare, a protégée of mine, who wants to go on the stage.'

Mr Annesley squeezed my hand most affectionately, and then answered. 'That is at once a very easy and a very difficult job, as doubtless you know, Madame Karl. Miss La Mare is very pretty and I am sure very clever but unfortunately that is not all that managers want. Has she seen anyone yet?'

I hesitated to speak of Lewis, but Madame took up the tale for me, and moreover told it with some circumstance and just a little exageration. The young man did not seem surprised, but he did not on the other hand seem very confident that I should find the agents much more demurely behaved.

It was suggested that we should lunch first; then I might make my visit to an agent Mr Annesley knew. The fat little man, Walker Bird, was awakened to make our party a square one, and we hansomed off to a place called Estlakes.

I had Walker Bird for my cab companion. I think the other man would have very much liked to have looked after me, but Madame captured him at once and he had no choice but go gently.

I expected the fat little man to improve the occasion, and he certainly did not disappoint me. The street was too open and the luncheon place so crowded that kissing was out of the question, but he made no bones about squeezing my hand affectionately.

I was glad when Mr Annesley said after lunch that I should come at once with him to see an agent.

Mr Rufus, the agent, inhabited the first and second floors of a house in the Strand. The doors on either side of his offices opened into bars, and about them were grouped numbers of shabby men whom no one would have any difficulty in recognising as actors. They all wore long coats, in some cases decorated about the collar and cuffs with fur of a very dubious origin, but in most cases extremely thin and bare. Within the bars I could see a number of ladies, whose costumes seemed to have been designed by an enthusiast of the kaleidoscope, and whose hats rivalled in their plumed splendor the paradise birds of the tropical regions. Their talk was loud and shrill, and could easily be heard in the street without.

'Chorus girls,' said Mr Annesley, laconically, 'they get thirty-five a week, and are expected to fill one of two stalls every evening, if they don't they get the sack, so you see they are in duty bound to get to know a lot of Johnnies.'

'Now then, Evans,' he said, to the young man in the outer office, 'I've brought a young lady who has to see Mr Rufus at once – at once, do you understand? Cut along in and tell him.'

In a few minutes the clerk returned with the message that Mr Rufus would see us directly. Presently a door swung open, and the excellent Mr Rufus appeared in person. For a moment, I thought that the poor man would be torn to pieces, for the attendant nymphs gathering up their skirts with one simultaneous and mighty rustle, like all the brown paper in the world being rolled up into a ball, bore down upon the devoted agent and besieged him with shrilly phrased interrogations.

As soon as we went to his room, he cordially welcomed Mr Annesley, but of me he took not the slightest notice; he did not even ask me to sit down, though he had comfortably buried himself in a large and well padded armchair. Mr Annesley began to explain the purport of our visit. It was barely finished, when Mr Rufus condescended to turn to me.

'Well, my dear,' he said, 'Mr Annesley speaks very highly of you, and your appearance is decidedly in your favour. You can read music at sight, I suppose?'

I nodded.

'And sing?'

I nodded again.

'Well,' he continued, 'you've just looked in at an opportune time. I've got to fill the chorus of a company that's just going out, and if you care to have the job, you can. Thirty shilling a week you begin on, but a girl like you ought not to stop long at that. Now, I shall expect you here at 11.30 on Monday to meet Mr Restall, the manager. Good-bye, Miss La Mare, you'd better get out this way, and if you like, when you come again, you can come up this back staircase; ring the bell at the bottom, and you'll be let in. Mind you, this is a special favour.'

I accepted the offer of the engagement; as a matter of fact, I had come prepared to accept anything, and left Mr Rufus by his private staircase. And so, in this way, I put my foot on the first rung of the dramatic ladder.

Annesley met me again outside, and asked me to have a drink with him. I wasn't very anxious to go into a public bar, but from what I saw of the ladies who were to be my theatrical companions, I gathered that it was a pretty usual thing to do. What would my reverend father, I wondered, have thought of his little daughter, had he watched her through the threshold of that glittering rendezvous?

We went into a small compartment, which we had to ourselves – in fact there was little room for anyone else there – and after a minute or two Mr Annesley remembered with a start that he had left his notebook in the agent's office. 'God forbid that anyone look into it,' he exclaimed, and then begged me to wait while he went back.

I could scarcely refuse, so sat perched on my high stool, sipping my whisky and soda, and watching as well as I could the flirtations of the pretty barmaids and the customers in the other little boxes. Suddenly I became aware of a low toned conversation in the next compartment to mine, and by reason of a crack in the dividing wall. I could hardly help hearing it.

The man talking were obviously actors, and their conversation dealt with the theatrical tours they had just returned from. I give it just as it came from their lips, bad language and all. It was a revelation to me; I had not supposed before that any class of men could be so utterly mean in giving away the secrets of favours received from the other sex.

Said actor No 1: 'How did you get on with the girls in your show? Had a pretty warm time, I suppose?'

'My word, they were hot ones,' was the answer. 'I started out meaning to live alone, but before two weeks, I had keeping house for me little Dolly Tesser.'

'I know her – pretty girl.'

'You're right; and you should see her with her clothes off, old man! A perfect peach, I can assure you. She was a bit shy at first, but I soon taught her all the tricks. My word, she is a bloody fine fuck!'

'Young, isn't she?'

'Oh, quite a kid, about seventeen – over the legal age though – you don't catch me making any mistake of that sort again. She wasn't a virgin, she'd been wrong with a conductor in the Gay Coquette crowd.'

'What, that syphilitic beast?'

'He hasn't got it really, but talking syph, have

you heard the tale of Humphreys and his land-lady's daughter?'

'No.'

'Well, he struck a place with an uncommonly pretty girl to wait. She was the landlady's daughter, and he hadn't been in the room three days before he was into her. Then on the fourth day, she didn't show up. He asked the old woman what was the matter.'

'Oh, Mary's very bad,' she said, 'we've had to send her to the doctor, he says she's got syphilis.'

'You can bet old Humphreys nipped round to the chemist pretty sharp, bought a bottle of black wash and kept bathing the old man all day. On the next day however, the old girl turns to him as she's taking away his breakfast and says: 'Oh, I made a mistake in what I told you about Mary yesterday, it is erysipelas.'

At that moment Annesley returned, so I was spared any more from the actors on the other side of the bar.

Annesley wanted me to go back to the office with him, but I was too excited at the prospect of my engagement and I wanted to hurry home to tell Madame Karl – but I did not get back.

It happened like this. There was the usual block to the Strand traffic at the bottom corner of the street, and, gazing idly out of my hansom, I saw a long haired poet whom I had met before. He saw me too, and fled recklessly through traffic to gain my side; he asked no invitation, but seating himself murmured: 'This is indeed a direct intervention of providence,' and told the cabman an address which I surmised to be that of his flat – it turned out to be so.

We drove rapidly down the Strand, and went down Arundel Street, in which street the poet said he had a nest that almost touched the sky. It certainly did, and as that particular block of buildings boasted no lift, it was a tired and panting little Blanche that at length gained the sixth floor. The poet apologised for the absence of the elevator, but immediately afterwards congratulated himself on none being there, for having a lift, he said, means also having a porter, and porters are horrid gossipy scandal mongering beings.

The front door passed, we found ourselves in a small hall, almost dark, save for the little light it gained from a heavily shaded electric globe which shed a discreet radiance upon an admirable painting of the Venus. A touch from the poet's fingers caused me to halt before the picture, and, as I gazed on it I felt his arms tighten round my waist, and his lips press gently upon my neck.

Here in this room was decadence indeed; all heavy curtains, little of the light of day, heavy scents again, and soft cushions everywhere. I sank down on a luxurious couch and waited events. He crouched at my side and began to kiss me; very slowly, but very deliciously and lovingly; his breath was scented with some pleasant Oriental flavour, a flavour which soothed my nostrils. Slowly his hand made its way over my calves and over my drawers; at the same time that he was feeling for the bare flesh of my thigh I was beginning to fumble with his buttons, and almost at the same moment that his fingers touched my clitoris, I had the naked flesh of his penis in my hand. It was very large and stout, a legacy of his north country parentage doubtless – and it throbbed amazingly.

For a few moments we felt each other without a word, overcome by our delicious sensations – and I made the next step toward a nearer intimacy by undoing his braces and buttons and sliding the front part of his trousers down till I could let my hand wander underneath his balls. That stung him into action. He freed himself from me, stood up and began to undress rapidly; in about a moment he stood before me stark naked and another moment saw me in the same condition.

We had only one fuck, but we lay there naked for hours, kissing and talking. I wanted more, and I hinted for it, but he would not. 'Another time, little girl,' was all he would vouchsafe. At last the falling shadows warned me that I must get back to Madame Karl, and I let him dress me. He gave me a little miniature on ivory of himself, and made an appointment for that day week, the day which coincided with my first rehearsal with the Restall Company. I made him get me a cab, and gave the Jermyn Street address. I felt full of lust as I sat back on the cushions of the hansom, and suddenly as we came into Trafalgar Square, the remembrance of the woman I had met that night of my first arrival at school, her invitation and her address came back to me. I recollected her promise to find me a dress, should I come to see her. Without further thought I pushed the trap and gave the driver her street and number.

3

I was put down before a plain-looking house in the midst of a row of equally plain looking houses. A pretty maidservant answered the bell, and seemed a little doubtful when I asked to see Miss Clarence, the name of my oddly met friend. However, my confident statement that I was expected, coupled, I dare say, with my generally smart appearance, ended in my being shown upstairs. I followed the maid to a large high-ceilinged room and at once recognised Miss Clarence in the lady stretched on an ample sofa.

She was got up in a most calculated negli-outer garment, but even that was cut low in gee. A semi-transparent tea-gown was on her shoulders and short in the arms like an evening frock, her knees were drawn up so that I saw her uncovered legs right up to well above the knee, uncovered that is, save for pretty openwork silk stockings of a greenish colour. She looked very attractive, her hair was obviously just done up by an artist in the coiffuring business, and she was beautifully made up. She had a cigarette in her lips and her left hand held a half emptied champagne glass.

There was a thick, intoxicating odour of scent in the room.

'Goodness gracious!' she said, after a prolonged stare. 'My little friend of two years ago; the girl just going to school. Well, it's a wonder I recognised you. Christ, you are altered, child!'

I mumbled that I had always remembered her invitation, but that this was the first opportunity I had had of accepting it.

'Well, you've come at quite an opportune moment,' she said, after she had extracted my story from me; how I had been cast off, and what had happened to me. 'I can make use of you this afternoon. I remember saying that you should have a dress, you shall have it.'

I didn't know very much of the world at that time, but I knew enough to realise that my hostess was a bad woman; bad, that is, in the sense of a woman who sold her body to a good bidder, and intuition taught me that she wanted me for the same purpose. Curiosity, and natural desire to make a little money, gave me courage. I was ready for pretty well anything.

She went on to tell me that she had arranged to find a virgin for one of her richest clients that very afternoon. The girl she had selected had disappointed her. 'In fact, my little dear,' she informed me, 'I was so much at a loss that I had got myself up as fascinating as possible to see if the old devil couldn't put up with me – now you've come.'

'But – ?'

'Exactly; you're not a virgin, but you look like

one, and the physical difficulties can be got over. You'll do very well for a first class virgin. First of all, however, that smart frock won't do; my old man expects a poor girl.' A ring at the bell interrupted her talk, and she immediately pressed an electric button at her side. 'Marie,' she said to the maid who entered, 'If that is General Salis, tell him to wait in the dining room. Give him a drink but don't dare to be loving to him or – '

'But the General is so impetuous,' answered the pretty girl.

'Well, don't let him put his impetuosity into you,' laughed Miss Clarence. 'Tell him that I have a little friend waiting for him.'

'Now,' she said when the girl had gone, rising to her feet, and becoming a businesswoman on the instant, 'are you game for this; it'll be ten pounds in your pocket; not a bad afternoon's earnings?'

'I'm game,' I replied. 'Give me a drink though.'

She poured out a glass of champagne, and while I was drinking it, began to undo my bodice. I was soon disembarrassed of everything but my underclothes, and Miss Clarence looked at me critically. 'Your undies are rather too smart,' she said, 'but I'll tell him I gave you these for the occasion. Now for the virginity part of the business.'

She led me into an adjoining room, filled a basin with water and dropped the contents of a paper into the water: 'That's powered alum,' she remarked, 'that'll dry your little cunt up, my false virgin,' at the same time filling a syringe with the mixture. I obeyed her and injected the alum and water. 'You'll have to bleed,' she added, 'these old men always look for that. I'll show you how. Here's a little bladder of pigeon's blood, put it under the string of your drawers, or anywhere else where you can hide it. When he's having you, you must wriggle about a lot and scream, and you must find a chance of breaking this. Crack it with your nail and manage to let some run over his cock and balls; get it into his hairy part if you can, but above all get your drawers saturated. If I know the General he'll probably want to take those away as a trophy; of course he'll give you extra money for another set for you.'

Then she dressed me up in a very plain three-quarter length dress of common material and made me let my hair down. 'Capital,' was her comment when she surveyed me, 'you don't look more than fourteen; the old man'll think he's got a treasure.'

With my little bladder of blood tucked into my drawers and my poor pussy dried up to the closing point with the alum, I followed her back into the drawing-room. She rang again, and presently the General followed the maid into the room.

It was a desperately business-like proceeding, and it was not till long afterwards that I recognised how all this straightforward bargaining and arranging appealed to the old rip for whom I made the sacrifice. She had instructed me to be extraordinarily coy, and I sat on the couch with my face half covered with my hands, taking care, however, to let the most attractive part of it be visible, and taking care at the same time to stick out my shapely legs as far as possible from under my frock.

The General was a fat man with a double chin and fierce moustache. He came into the room with a military stride, and kissed Miss Clarence on the cheek.

'Lock the door, Marie, and sit down by it,' said Miss Clarence, 'General – you trust me, and you must trust Marie – this child may be hurt, and I shall want someone to help me look after her.'

The old devil's eyes twinkled as he looked at me; became fiery lamps as I got up in obedience to Miss Clarence's gesture and suffered him to kiss me.

Miss Clarence was very business-like; in fact she was almost like a governess of a class and her manner was strikingly at variance with her alluring appearance, but how well she knew her man. He was boiling with excitement and anticipation.

'Now, General,' she went on, 'this girl is the daughter of a friend of mine. She is doing this for money because she is almost penniless. She has always lived in the country and knows nothing of men. I have told her what you are going to do to her, and it is the first time she has ever heard of any such thing.' The old reprobate, and I recognised him from his pictures in the papers as being a hero of the last war, was sitting on a couch, puffing a cigar and devouring me with his eyes while his ears followed Miss Clarence's introductory lecture. 'She is innocent, and has no idea of the value of her charms to mankind. You are going to pluck a very rare flower and you'll have to pay for it. Thirty pounds in all, General. Ten pounds for me, fifteen pounds for my little friend – you see how generous I am – and five pounds for Marie, who is staying here to help in any way she can. Is it a bargain?'

The old man rose to his feet? 'No, damn you it isn't!' he cried. 'It's a damned shame.'

'Well, why do you come here wasting my time?' snapped Miss Clarence.

'Thirty pounds for you, sixty for the girl, and a tenner for Marie,' blustered the General. 'I've just won an unexpected hundred pouunds on a horse this afternoon, and if the little lady wants money, damn she shall have it!'

The bargain, needless to say, was struck at once, and the General laid a roll of five pound notes on the table.

Then came my turn. I had been instructed by Miss Clarence to be perfectly passive and speak as little as possible. At her bidding I had laid myself out on the capacious sofa, and the old man approached. He kissed me lusciously several times, but I gave him no responding lips caress, and he then began feeling my legs. Miss Clarence and the maid were sitting, silent spectators, smoking cigarettes.

I wriggled and crossed my legs as he felt me, and pretended with little pushes, to thrust him away. 'Oh, damn it all, Bella,' I heard him say, 'I must have her clothes off!'

Bella Clarence pretended to whisper to me and gain my consent, and then disembarrassed me of all my outer clothes. I lay on the couch in my drawers and chemise, my long auburn hair flowing over my shoulders and breasts.

'That's enough off, General,' Miss Clarence said, 'You can't expect her to go stark naked the very first time.'

The General was a big, heavily formed man but his white hairs had led me to expect a very different instrument from the gigantic phallus that he produced. It was indeed a stout and powerful thing and reared up till its head almost knocked against his naval – he had stripped himself quite bare.

I gripped my little bladder of blood in my hand – and waited.

I shall never forget the scene at the commencement of the pseudo seduction. Above me towered the big old military man, and I remembered with a certain pride, as I felt him groping a way for his penis to my cunt, that he really was a very distinguished man. Behind him I saw Miss Clarence and the maid, beautiful women both, the eyes of both brightened with lustful curiosity, and the dainty room was a fitting box for its bawdy contents. I noticed my own pretty legs, and I drew them up to let the General get between them, and at last I felt the head of the General's penis trying to force an entrance.

The alum had dried me up, and the screams I

gave were by no means all theatrical. I felt some real pain until he had got well within me. Then joyous sensuality supervened, and it was with an effort that I remembered to slit the bladder with my nail and release the blood over his member, my legs and underclothes. When it was squeezed dry, I managed, introducing an elaborate fling of my arms, to the accompaniment of a frantic screech, to drop it behind the couch.

The General finished as he had begun, strongly; and filled me with a generous outpouring. I took it in with pleasure, and had some difficulty in raising the crocodile tears with which I was to shame him when he arose.

But my threatrical instinct triumphed, and my whole body shook with a spasm of sobbing when at last the old man drew his artificially blood-stained prick from within me and stood up.

'Well,' queried Miss Clarence, while the maid was sponging me between the legs.

'Magnificent!' answered the hero of Cathistan, glaring at his bloody cock and the sea of red fluid on my underclothes.

Miss Clarence gave me the sixty pounds, saying that my performance was worth far more than that to her, inasmuch as the General had been so pleased that he was sure to come again often, and send many friends. 'He was completely deceived,' she told me.

We went to dinner afterwards, and Miss Clarence insisted on taking me to the Majestic music hall.

We had to go through the Promenade at the

Majestic to reach our box, and I was astounded at the sight of the women loafing in the place. An atmosphere of lust filled the hall, and seemed especially to descend on the promenade. There was a set of well dressed, handsome girls, all agog to catch the attention of the men who idled, open eyed, calculating the value of the charmers, along the semi-circular Promenade. I knew of the existence of the women of pleasure, and I had heard the Majestic was a place frequented by them, but I had not expected such beauty, or nearly such numbers.

We spent a quiet evening. Only a brace of men came to chat with us in our box, and about eleven o'clock Miss Clarence decided to go home. I was too full of my new environment to wish to quit in a hurry, besides my sixty pounds burned in my pocket, and I was anxious to know more of a life that could offer such rewards for so little sacrifice. I said as much, rather gaily, to Miss Clarence, as the hansom was spinning westwards.

'Sixty pounds don't drop from the clouds often, my little one,' she said.

We had not gone very far on our journey before Miss Clarence volunteered the information to me that her best boy would be waiting for her at home. 'It's a treat I only give myself once a week,' she added, and asked me if I did not mind.

Of course I did not mind, and very soon the hansom brought us back to Mademoiselle Clarence's.

My friend's best boy was there, waiting for us, a handsome young animal of the hooligan type.

Villainy lurked in his eyes, and the low throwback of his simian-like brow; but my hostess was undoubtedly devoted to him, or at any rate to the animal part of him. She embraced him at intervals during supper, and the meal was hardly over before they were at it on the sofa, her costly evening dress thrown up anyhow round her breasts, and his ill cut trousers down to his knees. It was an odd contrast; the silken, scented finery of the smart prostitute mingled with the coarse clothes of the maquereau. Her legs were beautifully shaped, the dear, and her stockings of the finest silk gave their pretty curves every chance to be fascinating. His legs were good, too, what I could see of them, and very white. It appeared that he was a prizefighter by trade, and had to keep himself in the pink of condition. The hard, tense sinews of his thighs swelled up under the skin, and his bottom seemed altogether composed of muscles. As for that important weapon which seemed to give my friend such intense pleasure, it was really a formidable organ, long, large, and mightily stiff. The first fuck did not take long, but by the time Madame had spent, with a long drawn out sigh of satisfaction, I could feel something wet between my own little lily-white thighs.

Then they stripped and my abhorrence of the hooligan face was quite lost in my admiration of the body. He was splendidly made, and they were a beautiful pair; for she, though no longer in her first youth, had lost none of the contour and roundness of a really fine figure. Over and over they rolled on the big couch, first one on top and then the other, exciting each other to madness with every variety of love's tricks, and poor little Blanche grew very excited indeed. How I longed for that splendid prick in me, and I fancy that the young man longed to put it there too, for after the second bout was complete, he came and sat by me and laid a caressing hand on my leg. I offered not the slightest opposition, but Madame thought otherwise. She drew him away; 'No, no, you are only for me tonight, Billy,' she said.

I sighed: 'I think you two'll drive me mad.'

'Oh, you poor little dear, we must do something for you,' and together they undressed me, and laid me on the couch.

But there was no fucking for me – I was allowed to handle that member, feel it against my breasts, but Madame would not let him fuck me. She sucked me off, and so did he, and I rained kisses all over the two while they were fucking, at last sucking his cock while he kissed her pussy. And last of all, Madame sent for the maid to sleep with us. We were given a dildo, and told to make the best of that. It was something, but both the maid and I wanted that prick. Finally we went to the bathroom, conveniently adjacent to the bedroom, and washed out our hot and tired bodies.

We all slept together. Madame's bed was big enough to have accommodated Henry VIII and all his wives, and fell into a deep, utterly fucked, dreamless slumber.

I awoke first, found the boy next to me – we were all stark naked – and passed my hand over his body. His prick stiffened at the touch, and he awoke. He pressed his lips to mine, and despite the overnight orgies and the commonness of the man, his breath was sweet (that's the best of these athletes who don't smoke or drink, for he had had nothing the night before, through all that fucking) – rolled one leg over mine, and I was just preparing for a gorgeous fuck on the sly, when Madame awoke and pulled him from me.

'You must have thought me a selfish little beast,' she said afterwards, 'but he's my only extravagance, and I won't let him fuck another woman, whatever else he may do to them in my presence. I really believe he's absolutely true to me, as a matter of fact I think he has to be. I pay him well, and keep a damned good watch on him, he'd be a fool to lose me, and he knows well enough that if I found him out, his easy living would go.'

Madame made me promise to come and see her again, and insisted on making me a present of such a pretty nightdress, as a *souvenir d'amour*.

Madame Karl was naturally surprised, and not a little hurt, when I turned up in Jermyn Street looking absolutely washed out. I made a clean breast of it, and she ended by laughing and saying that I hadn't done so badly for myself. Madame Karl, it may here be appropriately mentioned, had in her younger days, when an apprentice at a great Parisian atelier, made a good bit of pocket money on her back.

Rehearsals with Restall proceeded smothly

enough, he liked me, and though his favouritism gained me a jealous look or two, the other girls did not dare to be openly hostile; besides, though I say it myself, I was a jolly, unaffected little kid, with no side, and ready enough to make friends.

I used to go out in the waits, to a scrappy lunch, or tea, with different male members of the company, but took care, acting on the advice of one of the girls with whom I had palled up, not to allow any familiarity on the part of the comedians – besides they weren't nice enough. The evenings I spent with Madame Karl, and we generally went to some theatre; I was anxious to see every play I could. As often as not Mr Annesley and little Walker Bird were our cavaliers, and one evening I shall never forget.

We had been, the night before, to a most admirable comedy, beautifully acted, but witnessed by a very meagre house. This night we had attended a popular burlesque, and had had the greatest difficulty in getting seats. We had supper in Jermyn Street and after supper Madame Karl said she would like to go to bed, she did not feel very well – but as she did not want to go to sleep, would we, after she was undressed, come and sit with her and chat.

We did. Madame looked as delightful as usual in bed; beautifully made up, exquisitely night-gowned, and under a becomingly shaded light. Annesley sat by her side, one arm around her dainty little waist, and the other apparently dangling by his side – he was on the blind side of the bed, so we could not see what exactly was employing those fingers, but Madame was wriggling every now and then.

The talk turned upon plays – Annesley held it a disgrace that what was really good in London should not attract. 'As for that trashy burlesque,' he said . . .

'Rot, oh rot, my dear fellow,' answered little Walker Bird, settling himself comfortably into an armchair. 'You may think it trash, though I know you've been at least a dozen times, but the public love it, and the public deserve to be catered to. Take the men in tonight's audience. They had worked hard during the day, and they had dined heavily when their work was over. They didn't want to think, their tummies were much too full. They wanted to laugh easily, and, above all, to see lots of pretty girls, and feel their old jocks stiffen,' – we four always talked very freely – 'and you bet your life they did stiffen tonight. Cunt, my dear Annesley, cunt, and lots of it, is what the greater part of this blessed nation wants. There's a certain proportion of the stalls who can take the cunt they see on the stage out to supper afterwards and block it, and a much larger proportion who wish they could, but who go home and block their wives or mistresses, instead. So everybody is satisfied, see?'

Mr Annesley must have got his finger rather farther than usual up Madame, for she wriggled furiously, then suddenly kissed him all over his face before he could reply – and when he did answer, he agreed with Walker.

Conversation lagged; Annesley was occupied

surreptitiously (as he thought) frigging Madame Karl, while I was getting hot as hell watching them, and Walker was getting hotter still, watching me. At last he got up and said he must be going. 'Don't hurry,' urged Madame Karl. 'I must,' answered Walker, but don't let me hurry you, Annesley, old chap.'

Annesley made no pretense of wishing to hurry, so I saw little Walker to the door.

In the hall he grabbed hold of me, thrust his tongue down my throat till I thought I should have choked, then begged me to let him have a piece.

Well, he got me into the shop, and there in the darkness, lit only by the furtive street lamp's ray or two that stole over the shutters, the little devil fucked me, on the shop table. He was a good long time about it, he had been drinking, but I quite enjoyed the performance. When it was over he kissed me fervently, wiped his cock with his perfumed handkerchief, exacted a promise that I would see him on the morrow, and departed.

I went up to Madame's room, and knocked. No answer. I went in on tip-toe. The bed clothes were thrown back, Annesley's trousers were down, Madame Karl's night dress was up, and Annesley's prick was half in her cunt but they were both fast asleep. I switched off the light, and tip-toed off again to my own little bedroom, where I undressed, admired my naked little self in the long glass, read a chapter from one of Madame's naughty books, tickled my clitoris a little, though not enough to come, and fell off into the land of dreams.

In the morning I woke up to find Madame by my side. She blushed when my eye met hers. 'Of course you know what happened last night, I could not help it. He's gone, got out before the servants were up.'

On the Thursday preceding the Monday we were to open at Oxford. Mr Restall, in a fit of sweetness towards me, produced I think by the generous effect of some very old, old brandy, asked me if I would care to go with him to a theatrical dance that same evening at the Harmonic theatre.

You bet I accepted. Dances were foreign to my experience, and the theatrical dances promised such gay and unusual experience that I literally jumped at the offer. He bade me look my best, and meet him for supper at the Alcazar Restaurant, opposite the Harmonic, at eleven thirty.

I was there at eleven thirty-five and had fifteen minutes in which to admire the frescoes on the wall.

Then Restall sailed in, to the accompaniment of much bowing and scraping on the part of the attendants, and a considerable addition to the civility shown me. I had been taken, I think, for a lady out on the pick up.

Restall, speaking and behaving in his usual restless, jerky manner, hustled me upstairs and found a table on the balcony.

The supper was a good one; but that is no great

matter in the present story. What I want to talk about is that theatrical ball, my first.

Restall liked my dress. I think at first, after he had invited me, he had suffered some doubt as to whether I, being only newly engaged, would turn up in a costume sufficiently worthy of him and the occasion.

But I think that the delicious confection presented me for the ball by Madame Karl not only reassured him, but even astonished him. He kept turning to look at me with obvious pride as we entered the Harmonic theatre.

The Harmonic was delightfully arranged for the occasion. The ballroom was of course the stage, enclosed in a woodland scene. At the back perched on a built up mossy bank, was the orchestra, and the pit usually occupied by the orchestra was filled for this occasion with flowering ferns, forming a hedge between the stage and auditorium. At intervals in the hedge were gaps, and through these gaps were gangways leading down into the stairs, much used as sitting out places by the dancers.

There were of course other sitting out places, and capital ones. The boxes for instance, the big ones on the pit and dress circle tier, though they were fairly easy to see into. Above them, much more private were the boxes on a level with the upper circle and still more delighful were the little boxes only designed to hold two, or at the most three, at the back of the dress circle. And you obtained a fair amount of privacy if you sat out in the gloom of the upper circle.

Restall was at once surrounded by a big crowd and after introducing me to one or two men, abandoned me at once. I was not destined however to linger as a wallflower; I attracted the attention with a nice big handsome gentleman and I was dancing to my delight.

Hardly a girl there that was not pretty, and nary a man who hadn't come to the theatre with the manifest purpose of enjoying himself; there was no duty business. All the girls were all well dressed, and none of them was chary of showing the most of their upper-work charms. I marvelled how some of them kept their bubbies within those dangerously décolleté corsages; I know that I myself had more than once to lift a guardian hand to keep my own nipples from overflowing on to the dress coat of my partner. Not that he would have minded, I dare say.

One man managed to knock down my fan, and was clever enough to get his hand just on to my stocking in the act of picking it up, but I kicked his errant fingers away, and the boy – he was one of the youngest guardsmen possible – blushed and apologised. I had to wait for my supper partner for anything serious to happen.

Walker Bird, who arrived precisely at the supper hour, brought him up to me, and so fascinated was I by his eyes, his figure, and his generally distinguished appearance, that I threw over the man I really should have supped with, without a second thought, and accepted unhesitatingly his suggestion that it was about time all of us felt a little hungry. Walker left us with a murmured, 'Keep a brace of pews for me and mine,' and caught us up at the door of the supper room — the big saloon bar transformed for the nonce into a palm embowered eating place — with a cute little chorister from the Harmonic on his arm. I recognised her in a tick, for were not her photographs in every print seller's window, and did not the evening papers keep stock headlines going for her breach of promise cases? She had on a dress worth at least a hundred pounds, and she greeted me simply, after the introduction, with 'Lord, you could at least speak a bit.'

I supped gaily and well; the wine was exhilarating, the food first rate; the surroundings the gayest, and I had my supper partner's leg entwined round my left, and Walker's left leg round my right. It was a round table, and I have no doubt that the little chorister was being endeared in precisely the same manner. We had a quartette of Tsiganes for a separate supper orchestra, and their strains made my little head swim with naughty thoughts. All at once I felt I was sitting on something wet, and I knew that I had come involuntarily, so much so that I welcomed our little friend's suggestion after supper that we should go and put a puff on.

We were alone in the retiring room — 'Gay ain't it old dear?' she said, as she drew a stick of red across her pretty little mouth, and then passed it on to me — 'makes me feel hot as hell,' she passed her hand up her dress, 'I thought as much,' she pursued, 'I've spent — what a bleeding waste.'

In one of the WC's I took the chance of wiping

my underclothes as dry as possible, for I was in that stage of full-bloodedness that I was absolutely determined to have a man that evening – even if I had to ask for it. And so much were the faces of the men altered since supper that I didn't think that event at all probable.

Near the door I found my supper partner and he led me at once into a valse, a deliciously suggestive thing, admirably rendered by the band. He too, was mad for a woman. There was no disguising that fact, for through my dress I could feel his swollen prick pressing against me, he had arranged it up his trousers, pointing to the navel – and I should say very nearly touching that spot, in the careful manner of the man wearing evening dress who realises that he is likely to be overcome by the outward and visible sign of his manhood – and I don't deny that my little tummy pressed back.

We both danced well, both recklessly and with abandon, and whether it was that the other couples admired our performance so much that they wanted to witness it, or whether the other girls were nervous of becoming an obstacle to our wild career, at any rate we pretty soon had the floor to our own selves. I heard several complimentary remarks as we whirled by, and once I caught Restall's eye full, it bespoke admiration, and by the motion of his lips as he turned to speak to the man by his side, I had an inkling that he was informing the man of the fact that I was a member of his company, and that he, Restall, intended to sleep with me. He could have had me then and there if he had chosen to come and ask, and provide a place.

The music stopped suddenly, and my partner and I sank exhausted on to the nearest seat. As he fanned me, he whispered: 'This is an uncomfortable sitting out place. I know one much better – shall we go?' and I only nodded my answer.

'This is the place I mean,' he said, when we paused before a curtained door, situated near the stage. He drew the curtain aside, and next minute I found myself in a cozy little room, and heard behind me the unmistakable sound of a key being turned in the lock.

The room was furnished mainly with a large sofa, the sort that has the ends made to flop down, and a number of theatrical photographs. I thought it was some sort of private sitting room, had I known more I should have guessed at once that it was a dressing room. The photographs of the celebrities were mostly women, and all signed.

As there was no other place to sit on I flopped on the sofa at once, and a moment later my partner was at my side, his arm tight around my waist, and his lips on my cheek.

I suppose it was the fact of my clerical descent that made me leap to feet with a little noise of disapproval when I felt his fingers tickle the bare flesh above my petticoats, or was it the fear that some one might come in? – at any rate he took it for the latter, for he hastened to assure me that the door was locked.

'But,' I replied, still rather coy, 'suppose anyone should want to come in and sit out in this room, too?'

'That they're not likely to do,' he said, with a delicious smile, 'for you see this is my dressing room.'

Then I recognised him, he was the tenor of the Harmonic company but the absence of the small pointed beard he affected on the stage altered him, for the better I think.

'I saw you in a box a little time ago,' he said. 'You looked like a little dream, but you were with society people. How do you come to be here, and brought by Restall?'

I didn't care that evening; I was carried away by surroundings, and the man seemed so nice, so I told him a good deal of the story (always mind you, my readers, suppressssing that fact that George Reynolds had actually pierced my little bird's nest – as Walker Bird is in the habit of calling those inner temples of Venus in which he from time to time inserts his chubby little prick) and his embrace was so comforting, and I suppose I wanted it so much, that I made not the slightest demur when once more he placed his hand beneath my clothes, slid up my silk stockings and eventually laid it on my Mons Veneris.

He slid quietly to the ground, pulled me gently forward till my little bottom just balanced on the edge of the sofa, all the time lifting up my clothes with his other hand, and then pressed himself against me.

'*Half a mo –* ' *interrupted Gladys – she gets shock-*

83

ingly suburban when she's excited – 'Do you mean to tell me, you little simpleton that you actually let the man fuck you with your new ball dress on?'

And I had to confess to Gladys that in my innocence I actually did do such a silly thing.

'The man ought to have known better – and a well known actor, you say. Actors I've fucked have been most considerate about my clothes, but go on and get to the fucking.'

First fucks with different men are, I suppose, all more or less the same; unless, of course, the man is some old beast, or ugly, or with a dirty beast you are only doing it for money. With a many you want to fuck, the excitement is so great, and you begin to come so soon, that you really haven't any time to notice whether he does it artistically or not; it's seldom, indeed, that you even distinguish any great difference in the size of his penis from the man you had last. At any rate my friend, I did not even know his name, got into me till I could feel his balls hang against my bottom, and spent very quickly. He kept it right in me and fucked me again slowly and deliciously, and I can tell you I was in a bit of funk of having been put in the family way when at last the sense of joy had passed, and I stood up. He was sitting opposite me in a chair, his penis perfectly limp.

'Well, I suppose we'd better be getting back,' he said, after I had arranged my dress as well as I could, 'people'll be looking for you.'

I thought at first that he was callous; sufficiently pleased to have had a new girl, and wanted to be rid of me. I was angry – but when I suggested leaving him, he would have nothing of it. He took me into one of the first tier boxes, where we sat and watched the other dancers.

Willie Moorfield knew his way about London, and I spent quite an amusing evening while listening to his running comments on the celebrities present.

Miss Marion Storm, the successful comic opera prima donna of two continents, floated by on the arm of a very nice young man, who looked as near to being made up as any young man I had ever seen before. He was, so said Moorfield, a young gentleman who liked being an actor, and with whom audiences put up because it was general knowledge that he had only four or five consumptive and syphilitic cousins between himself and an Earl's coronet. He loved notoriety, and was at the present moment paying assiduous court to Marion of the nut brown hair, tip-tilted nose, and generally fascinating and devil may care expression, because he knew that a lot of other men in London wanted her; that, in fact, she was the fashion.

'They say he really means to marry her – or rather she's quite determined that he shan't get out of it,' said Moorfield, 'I only hope they won't both fall in love with the same man.' Which rather amazing statement left me with the idea that the Honourable Mr George Danvers, Clarendon, Hope, Travis, Gwyn Iumthait was by way of real inclination – a sod.

'*Don't you think you're getting rather vulgar, Blanche?*' *this from Gladys.*

'*You mean in my words? Well, I don't agree with you, and anyway, a sod is a much nicer term than bugger, which old Doctor Johnson so delightfully describes in his dictionary as "a term of endearment, common among sailors."* '

But I mustn't waste time. Moorfield went on to tell me that Miss Storm had ruined almost as many men as Belero, and was equally proud of the fact. Married originally to a comedian, far, at that time, above her own station, both socially and professionally, she had thrown him over without the slightest compunction when fortune began to smile on her, and a man with a bit of money came her way.

The man with a bit of money took a theatre for her; procured a play for her, and made her in the twinkling of an eye one of the greatest stars of the burlesque stage in England. Her salary went up, she became the rage, but the man with the money lost it over the venture. 'It was only the other day,' said Moorfield, 'that she met him at Ostend, as she was leaving the boat. He was broke to the world, and the opportunity of the custom house business gave him the chance to ask her if she could lend him a tenner or so. She put half a crown on the douane counter, and turned her back. And that night, too, she slept with an actor who hadn't a sou to his name, and who, more than likely as not, borrowed a cool hundred from her.'

'She has money, and she is an artist to the heels

of her little shoes,' continued Moorfield. 'But she has the lust of money, and whoever the man may be, provided he can give her any more, she will fuck him for it. She will marry that ennobled descendant of a complacent Stuart prostitute and despite the twenty thousand a year he can give her, she will go on acting, because she likes it, loves it for itself, and likes the fame and applause it brings her, and she will go on fucking, because she likes that too, and because, however much money she has, she glories in earning more by her cunt.'

'I gather,' says Gladys, 'that you and your new friend had become pretty intimate – to judge from your language.'

Well, gentle readers, we had. A sort of affinity seemed to have sprung up between us – and we glided into using dirty words just as if they had been the ordinary common talk of polite conversation.

Little Annabel Cupid was the next goal of his spiteful tongue: he hadn't much to say of her save that she wasn't able to suck a man off because she feared that the enamel on her face would crack.

Of Madame Sydney, the operatic star, he told me that she had an absolute passion for loose life, but that she feared so much to find herself enceinte, that she would only play the sucking game with her lovers, or allow them to make an entrance up her stage door.

'The dirt road, as the Americans call it,' interrupts the conscientious one.

'*Americans are dirty people.*' I say.

'*And have you ever – ?*' but at that moment we hear the door open, and our dear old Baron comes into the room.

Interlude with the Baron.

He enters with that assumption of youth which long experience has taught me to know that the old boy feels like it, salutes first myself and then Gladys with cheery kisses, hands us each a bunch of rare flowers, and squats down contentedly on my big window seat – 'You're interrupting, as usual, Baron,' I say.

'If I may only make some trifling compensation?'

'I really begin to think that the only punishment we can inflict, is to put him into the book, right name and all,' this from Gladys.

'I have lunched so well and I feel so nice and I know so well that there is not such company in London as can be found here, may not that be an excuse?'

We try for a little to go on with the work, but the old man is always anxious to put his arm round my waist or to look over Gladys' shoulder to see how she is getting on, and the work doesn't go on at all.

'I see you are writing about Sodomites,' he chuckled.

'Yes,' answers Gladys, savagely, 'Aren't you one?'

The old dear man wasn't angry, but proceeded there and then to talk volubly about the particular sect of young and old gentlemen who prefer connection with their own sex to the ordinary channels provided in the female kind by wise dispensation of providence.

'You should see the sods as you call them,' he began, 'and the word reminds me of a dear old friend who proposed to insult a gentleman who had behaved in that way with his youngest son, my friend's youngest son, that is. He left a card at the bugger's club, with the inscription, "You are a Sodomite." And it wasn't till a day afterwards that he remembered he had put two "d's" in the middle of sodomite. It upset him terribly.'

'I suppose you know the tale, Baron,' says Gladys, 'of the New York young gentleman of that persuasion who walked delicately, like Agag, into a New York saloon and asked, 'Is my friend Sweet Evening Breeze here?'

'No,' replied the bartender, 'He's locked up.'

'Oh dear,' said the young man, 'what for?'

'Cock sucking.'

'Thank God, it's not for theft.'

The Baron laughed. 'After all,' he said, 'I suppose it all seems very disgusting to you girls, but sometimes an old roué feels the need of something new.'

'That may be,' says Gladys, 'but as for what you call buggery, I for my part, don't believe it's possible. I know no man could get up me that way.'

'You remind me rather of the eminent CO my dear Gladys,' answers the Baron, 'the CO who said it was practically impossible to obtain a

89

conviction against a prisoner for that particular offense, because, one half of the jury do it themselves, and the other half don't believe it's possible.'

'I am still a female Didymus,' says Gladys.

'Shall I prove it?' asks the Baron.

'If you like,' says Gladys.

'With your permission, Madame Blanche?' queries the Baron.

I nodded, really thinking that the old man was joking, but he immediately produced a fountain pen, and sat down at the writing table. When he had finished a brief note, he asked me if I could have it sent.

'But Baron?' I murmured, hesitatingly.

'It's perfectly right, my dear Blanche. Your friend doubted the existence of sodomy, and I am going to prove it to her that it does exist. This note will bring two chaps, adepts at the game.'

'But,' I interposed again, 'isn't it rather dangerous?'

'Certainly not. The lads are as discreet as the tomb; it pays them to be. They need not know that this is your house; they will probably think that it is a place I have taken.'

'And what sort of people are they?' asks Gladys.

'Singers, both of them.'

'Isn't it bad for the voice?' I asked.

'Actual sodomy perhaps is, but sucking off is wonderful, as I dare say you know, my dear Blanche?'

I did know. Earlier in my career I had the tip

from Madame Sydney, the famous soprano. She kept two fine young men for that very purpose, and every night before fulfilling an important engagement, she sucked one or the other, sometimes both, to a finish. She regarded male semen as the finest possible lubricant for the vocal chords. I took her advice with good results. It's much nicer than voice medicines, and I dare say, many of you dear little comic stars and music hall artists who read and get naughty over this immortal work can bear me out. Take my advice, dears, and if, in a pantomine, you get jealous because one of the comedians is going too well, suck him off; his performance will lose, while yours will gain in proportion.

The Baron's men arrived in about half an hour. Gladys and I had discreetly masked our pretty faces, but masked very little else, for we had both begun to feel very randy, and had employed the waiting interval by making the old man lick our pouting pussies. When the boys were shown in by my confidential maid they found two pretty women lying on their backs on the big rug with bare legs, also bare cunts; temptingly displayed.

They were charming young men, both about twenty-two, and sweet and fresh to look at. The Baron kissed them both on the lips, and told them to begin at once.

They undressed stark naked. Such nicely formed white-skinned bodies they had, and firm pricks, no preliminary dalliance being wanted to make them rise. The entertainment began with sucking, first one man sucking the other, and then both playing sixty-nine. But Gladys was anxious for the action, so the first one was bent over the back of the sofa, his arse distended for the reception of the other's weapon.

'We shall want vaseline,' hazarded the second boy.

'Nonsense,' said Gladys, rising to the occasion, 'this will do.'

With that she placed her finger in her cunt, which was over-flowing with juice, and annointed them.

It did do, for the prick slid in easily. A few wriggles on the part of the subject, and then the weapon was right inside him and up to the hilt. The subject seemed to enjoy it thoroughly, for his prick grew stiff as a ramrod, so beautifully stiff that Gladys could not resist fondling it. A few frantic strokes, a quiver, and the fellow withdrew his cock, dripping with spend. It was done; Gladys had seen an act accomplished which could have cost either of the two performers imprisonment for life.

The Baron turned to us with the air of a successful showman. 'Ladies,' he said 'You once or twice laughed at my inability to complete the act of fornication; if one of you will assist me, I will soon show you now that I do it.'

And this is how he did it; Gladys, her legs apart, was stretched on the big rug, the Baron knelt between her thighs, and the chap whose prick still remained stiff got into the old man from behind. At once his withered cock stiffened, and in two shakes of a duck's arse, as the vulgar proverb has it, he had slipped down on to and into Gladys. The boy thrust, the Baron fucked, and Gladys wriggled. All of them very soon came; but the boy withdrew and the Baron got off the panting Gladys with a little grunt of triumph.

All were satisfied; all that is, save poor me, who had had nothing – but eventually I had the best of it. The men washed their cocks in rose-scented water. I took one dear cock in my mouth, and the other up my back (it was not my first experience – but that is another story). I made the Baron suck my cunt but let me explain the position – I knelt and lay forward with the fellow I was sucking underneath me. The Baron was also underneath me. With one hand I fingered the Baron's prick and with the other felt Glady's cunt. Gladys had her roving commission. One of her dear, soft little hands wandered over my body, and the other tossed off the man I was sucking – thus everybody came in four distinct ways. I had a cock in my mouth which was delightfully stiff, yet not too big. (Big cocks give you cramp in the jaw muscles) I had a cock exactly the right size up my bottom, and any girl who has been had that way knows the joy that is. My cunt was being licked by an expert in the art, and a dear girl was feeling my bosom, likewise I had the pleasure of tickling a cock with one hand and a cunt with the other. It was a pretty group. I could see it all in a mirror, and I only wish we could have had it photographed. We continued for about ten minutes, till every one concerned had spent, even including the Baron – it took about a pint of old, old brandy to pull him straight afterwards.

Gladys, who had watched the boy doing me, had noticed that I enjoyed it very much, now had the presumption to express her opinion that she could take a prick up her back door. So she knelt on the rug, and one of the men placed his weapon at the entrance. He had a hard time of it, and wasted some little time getting into her virgin rosette, but with the aid of some saliva, at last got all the way into her, and I think she enjoyed it immensely.

One of the last acts in the comedy was a more simple one, savouring indeed somewhat of the diversions of our sailors when far from land. The Baron put up a five pound note as a prize for which fellow could come first. My man, I am pleased to say, won hands down, thus once more exemplifying the old proverb that experience will tell. He spent with a scream of delight, occasioned, no doubt, by the mixed joy of the action and the reflection that his feat had earned him five pounds.

Subsequently we all sat down to a light refreshment of tea, cakes and champagne – all naked as we were.

Gladys and I, to round off the party, had another go at this new sport. She seemed to have taken quite a delight in this form of fornication. While her fellow was working away in her rear parlor, Gladys wriggled her arse like a fairy. The old Baron laughed uproariously at her antics, and twitted her about her previous remark about her tight little arsehole that no man could get into — offering to bet that even he could get into her now.

After a short rest Gladys let him try it, at the expense of a diamond ring, and he soon succeeded in shoving his big joystick up in her pooper, causing her to squeal with rapture.

4

But to return to the earlier history of Blanche La Mare, so scandalously interrupted by the Baron and his lusty lads.

I will skip all further details of my life in London till the Herbert Restall Company got away on tour. We were to open at Oxford and the 'train call' was for Paddington, 11:30 of one memorable Sunday morning. I turned up early, unaccompanied, for Madame Karl had gone out to supper the night before, and had not returned – perhaps as a little revenge for my absences.

Still, I was not the first on the platform, and I soon got to learn that the habit of theatrical companies was to arrive very early at the station, and exhibit their best frocks. I had my best frock on, and I'm certain it was the best in the company. Herbert Restall cast an admiring glance at me when he arrived. He did not speak to me, and I noted the reason. His wife, an angular lady past fifty, and of a forbidding and non-conformist type of countenance, followed him everywhere.

We had a special train from platform number

three, and I was engaged in looking for it, when Annesley appeared.

'Madame Karl is so sorry she couldn't get back,' he apologised, 'but her cousin was ill, and – .'

'Never mind the explanations,' I cut him short. 'I hope you both enjoyed yourselves.'

To judge from the lines under his eyes, he had.

He found me the train, and he found me also the acting manager, who was engaged in gumming labels on the carriage windows; labels indicative of the compartments to be occupied by various members of the company. Thanks to Annesley's introduction, I was not put to travel with the chorus ladies, but with the two 'Sisters Knock', the dancers, to whom also Annesley introduced me, and we all repaired to the bar together in which pleasant spot were assembled the majority of the company, some seventy all told.

To Annesley's introduction I owed a pleasant journey, for the two sisters Knock turned out jolly companions, and very soon threw off any reserve. I produced my cigarette case, and conversation very soon became not only general, but free.

They were neither of them girls who made the slightest pretence of being moral; they took it for granted that I was the same. They were pretty girls, hopelessly uneducated and common, but possessing a certain subtle gaminerie that gave them an odd charm of manner. They were dancers, wherefore it is not necessary to do more than state that their figures were excellent. They were absurdly alike, in face, figure, eyes, hair and everything and by dressing alike, down to the very smallest detail, they made it difficult for anyone but their most intimate friends to tell the difference. Once, when I knew them better, I ventured to remonstrate with them on this point.

'You must at least make a point of helping people to decide between you.' I said.

But the eldest Miss Knock, who was generally the spokeswoman of the two, was not at all of my way of thinking. 'My dear stupid little darling,' she opined, 'that's exactly why we keep the deception up. We don't want people to know the difference. Now, barring that Maud's got a bit of a mole on her left hip which I haven't, we're just about as alike as two peas.'

She helped herself out of a generously sized flask, passed it round, and settled down to be confidential.

Then she went on to tell me how useful it was when either she or her sister had an engagement with a man that they couldn't keep. It appeared that no man could tell them apart, even in bed, and even when quite undressed and in strong light. All that Maud had to do when her sister sent her in her place was to put a bit of gold beater's skin over the tell-tale mole, and things were all Sir Garnet. In fact Maud once went to Paris for a week with a new mash of Mabel's, while Mabel stopped at home to see after a rich American whom she had just picked up. If it hadn't been for that convenient sister she would have had to forego either the American or the other boy, which could have meant a loss of money. Mabel was the best talker of the two, and it was generally she who first attracted the men, but which sister the men got afterwards, when matters had been arranged, was simply a matter of chance. The girls went shares in all they got, and they did very well. Likewise, to mention a very intimate matter, it came in particularly useful when one of the two happened to be incapacitated from love by the presence of her monthly periods. The other simply filled the vacancy. Mabel collared quite a sum of money on one occasion, it appeared, by wagering with a rich young sportsman that she would take fifteen men twice each, during a night of eight hours, and come every time. Now she was game for fifteen, being a girl of exceptionally amorous and capable temperament, but double that amount was naturally beyond her. So the arrangement was made that the tourney was to take place in her own flat, and that she was to be left alone for a while between each insertion.

Of course you can guess that sister Maud, of the existence of whom the men were unaware, stepped into the gap on alternate occasions, and the deed was triumphantly accomplished and the money won, two hundred and fifty pounds, quite a nice little doucer for the two.

I believe it was a delightful ceremony. The young man who made the bet brought fourteen of his friends, and they were Sandhurst boys in the very pink of health and physical strength, and right lustily they accomplished their task.

The whole affair was very well managed, I gathered from Mabel's narrative. The boy who proposed the bet was rich, and he presented the performers with a supper amply calculated to in every way feed their lust. Likewise a sideboard groaned to sustain the men and the greatly daring girl during the night.

The first supper was decorous enough, for Mabel refused any early advances on the part of the men. A few bawdy toasts were drunk and Mabel made to swear a solemn oath that she would not lie about coming. Supper over, the devoted girl retired to her room, which led out of the dining room, and returned stark naked. And a pretty sight she must have been, exciting indeed to the eyes of those randy young men. I have often seen her naked in the dressing room, for she was one of those girls who have no scruples about exposing herself naked to the gaze of others of the same sex, and I always admired her.

The men drew lots for order of performing, the proposer of the bet, however, reserving to himself the third turn, which he reckoned would be the best. That settled, Mabel let the way in to the bedroom, arranged herself on the luxurious bed, and called to the first man to come on and do his damndest. He stripped, a muscular young giant of nineteen, blushing a little at the unaccustomed publicity of his act, and was into her without further ado. He had given but three or four vigorous thrusts when the dear girl cried out that she had come and forced him to get off her. There was no doubt about the coming; the hero of the wager introduced his finger into the well greased aperture, and abundantly satisfied himself. Then arose a difficulty. Mabel asserted that the act of her coming constituted the completion of the fuck, but the only half satisfied young man naturally asserted that he had an equal right to finish his share of the business. After some argument the poor girl had to agree that he had, and, though she offered to suck him instead, he remounted, and finished, making her come once more before it was done.

Then the assembly filed out into the next room, leaving Mabel alone. She was to ring a handbell when next prepared.

Of course Maud, her gold beater's skin concealing the mole, was produced out of a cupboard, whence she had viewed the proceedings and gathered all the conversation, so that she should not be found forgetful of any subject that might have been broached. The men were not a little astonished to hear the bell go almost immediately after their departure, and then were still more astonished to witness the vigorous lust that the psuedo Mabel displayed.

It was only a question of a few frantic strokes and the second hero and Maud united their spending and obviously completed the fuck.

She went back into the dining room with them to take a little refreshment. 'Maud,' so Mabel told me, 'was ever the drinking one of the two.' She then retired, and in five more minutes the bell rang for the third man who quite unexpecting so speedy a gratification of his lusts had not begun to undress.

And so the game went on, first Mabel and then Maud rising to the occasion, till all the men had had their first go within less than two hours from the start.

After that Mabel – she did practically all the talking – bargained for a couple of hours sleep, which was granted her. At the end of the two hours, she was awakened. Maud, poor thing, had had to put up with the narrow limits of an armchair in the cupboard all that time, and the contest began anew. The girls worked so well that there were but two fucks to be completed when there still remained two hours of the alloted time to run. At that juncture Maud nearly failed. Instead of profiting by the time limit to have a good rest, she pronounced herself ready directly after Mabel had taken the twenty-eighth cock.

When her young man had finished, and he was not unreasonably quick about it, he asked her if she had come, in compliance with the regulations. She, being a straightforward girl, was bound to reply that she had not. The question then arose whether the man who just finished, being incapable of immediate continuance, another might take his place. Maud protested that she could do it, if only the man was not in such a hurry. Eventually it took four of them, one after the other, each working their hardest, while Maud herself made herself naughty by imagining the depraved things, before the blessed dew anointed the lips of her cunt.

It was perhaps bad policy, but Mabel could not resist the opportunity for working a considerable surprise. Almost directly after the fatigued Maud had washed herself and retired into the cupboard, she walked out into the sitting room, quaffed a glass of champagne, and announced herself ready for the last man. He mounted her there and then in the room and they came together in about two minutes.

Then the cheque was handed over, and so ended a surprising evening.

When we arrived at Oxford I was undecided where to stay; being quite in ignorance of theatrical tours and living arrangements, I had intended to go to a hotel. Certainly my salary was only thirty-five shillings a week, but I had a little spare cash. The genial sisters Knock, however, quickly disabused me of that. 'Come and stop with us, old dear,' they said, 'don't go putting up at hotels and making folks think you're a tart before they can prove it,' – and I went.

The rooms were rather a shock. Small and meanly furnished – the mural decorations consisted of a religious tract and lithographs, and the landlady was as dirty as she was familiar. But the sisters seemed to think they were in clover. 'Old Ma Osborne's a bit of all right,' explained one of the sisters, 'doesn't mind who we have in, or what we do, and that's saying something in a place like Oxford.'

When the question of dinner was mooted, old Ma Osborne grinned, 'Well me dears,' she said, 'I haven't worried about getting you any dinners, because knowing you like and your habits, I've took the liberty of telling Lord Hingley of the House, which is Christ Church College, me dear, that he might be at liberty to call. And Lord Hingley, me dears, will see as how you have a better dinner than I might be able to offer you here.'

I was inclined to be annoyed, but held my peace.

Maud Knock (the one with the mole) became business-like at once.

'Many thanks, I'm sure Mrs Osborne,' she said, 'but who is Lord Hingley, he's not on my visiting list?'

'Is he all right?' chipped in the moleless sister, 'none of your courtesy title paupers, eh, what?'

'All right; that I would say he is. Ten thousand a year he has, as I should know, dearies, my husband being his scout for nigh on two years in college, and as generous a gentleman as ever was.'

The sisters Knock nodded assent, and Ma Osborne retired beaming.

The highly recommended Lord Hingley presently made his appearance accompanied by his friend, Mr Charles Latimer; apparently they had only reckoned on two, and I saw breakers ahead, for, without conceit, I knew well enough that neither of the sisters could hold a candle to me in looks, or in any sort of attraction.

We were conveyed in cabs to Mr Latimer's

room. Mr Latimer was a rich young gentleman, son of the famous brewer of that name, and he occupied the most elegant apartments. He was plain but well groomed, and very well dressed. Despite his origin he was a gentleman. Lord Hingley was nice looking, if rather stupid, and obviously too fond of drink. They were both scrupulously polite to us girls. We had a most admirable dinner, cooked and served in a style which would not have disgraced a smart west end restaurant, and we all of us drank rather too much champagne, to say nothing of subsequent liqueurs. Still nothing happened, and the men made no attempt at love-making. The sisters obliged at the piano, so did I, and after I had done so, Lord Hingley contrived to get me alone in a corner.

'I say,' he stammered, 'you're a lady, aren't you?'

'I'm certainly not a man.'

'But, don't joke; you aren't like the others. How did you come to be living with Maud and Mabel?'

'Because they are my friends.'

The poor boy became very nervous, so I explained.

'I am a lady by birth, but who I am and how I came to be here, I don't care to have anybody know. If I told you my father's name, you would probably know,' that was a good bluff considering the name was the same as my stage name – poor old Pop La Mare – 'so don't ask.'

But he squeezed my hand; not as a man would

squeeze the hand of a chorus girl tart, and I knew that he was in love, the first young man or title who had loved me. He likewise made an appointment for the following day, to meet at the Queen's Restaurant for lunch, subsequently a drive, and a hasty little dinner at his own rooms to follow – (he lived out of college).

I went down to the theatre on the following morning – the first time I had entered a theatre as a member of a theatrical company, and early as I was, several of the girls were there before me, and the best places in the dressing room, which was to contain six of us girls, were taken.

There were the twin sisters Knock, Lily Legrand, a show lady of more or less mature age, but undeniable charm of figure, and little Bertha Vere, Restall's mistress, who was not, however, allowed any special privileges in the company because of her relationship to the 'Guvnor'. I had to hang my clothes up in the middle of the room, and do without a looking glass. My brand new make-up box occasioned great joy among the other girls, who all appeared to have come with the tiniest remnants of the necessary powders and pigments.

My first day in Oxford, also my first day on tour, was fairly uneventful, I went out to lunch with my lordling friend, but he treated me with extreme courtesy, to say nothing of a very good lunch. I found out afterwards that Oxford boys, while always delighted to get to know any actress on the road, yet expect little in return for their hospitality. My young man did not even attempt to kiss me, though we sat for a long time in his rooms after lunch – I think that he was even rather shocked that I smoked.

When I got back to my lodging I found the sisters Knock there, back also from a luncheon party. They had brought on my letters from the theatre. One of them was from the poet, and of a distinctly improper nature. Its pretty indelicate imagery, and a most sensual drawing by an artist friend which was enclosed, brought so much moisture on my legs that I had to get upstairs and wash before I dared face the semi-public undressing of the theatre dressing room.

As the majority of the company had appeared in 'The Drum Major' before, we had no dress rehearsal, and I had not even seen my costumes till I got to the theatre that night. 'The Drum Major' was a tights play and all the girls in our room wore those fascinating garments. I was rather anxious to see how the legs of the other girls looked. Mine I knew, were all right, a little on the small side perhaps, but quite perfectly modelled. I could submit to the difficult task of inserting a three-penny piece between my naked thighs when placed together, and keeping it there. I had also silk tights, a present from Mr Annesley, who had informed me that the management considered cotton good enough for the chorus. He had found out the colour of my dresses, and had these made for me.

The girls in the room displayed little delicacy. Maud undressed stark naked, and walked about the room rubbing herself down with a towel. Her figure was good. Shapely legs, if perhaps a little too muscular to satisfy the artist who takes his ideal from the ancient Greek statues, but that was the fault of her dancing training. A firm, rather brownish skin, but without wrinkles, she wore no corsets, and round breasts with scarlet nipples. Her arms were also muscular, and she had the hair under her armpits shaved off, though a great abundance of dark and luxurious moss curled round the lips of her cunt and blossomed up on to her stomach.

Lily Legrand kept her vest on while putting on her tights, not omitting, however, to show the hair on the lower portion of her body, and the sexual organ underneath. Mabel Knock stripped boldly to the buff and displayed a figure which was almost an exact counterpart of her sister's, but she was more modest, and turned her back on us while she hurriedly slipped into her tights. Little Bertha, Restall's mistress, was far more discreet, and got into her leg attire under cover of other garments. The reason for that was, I afterward discovered, that she padded. I was also as modest as might be, and immediately aroused the suspicion of the eldest Knock girl that I had come to the theatre with my pads on, a common enough practice with some chorus girls who are ashamed of letting their companion tarts know that nature had not been altogether kind to them. She took me by surprise, and ran her hand all over my legs. 'Genuine,' she pronounced, with a laugh, and Bertha looked envious.

It was a military play and I was one of the

officers, and I had practically to open the show with five others, headed by our captain, a very dapper little lady who was the principal boy of the play. When I first walked on to the stage, I could hardly see for fear (luckily I was placed last). I felt practically naked and the music surged in my ears and it was only when I heard the other girls break into the surging melody of the song that I regained enough self-possession to join them. However, in half an hour I was all right, and got the brace of lines allotted to me off swimmingly.

The piece went well; Restall was in great form, and was ably backed up by his leading lady, a well known exponent of soubrette parts. In the third act he was at his very best, but I had an awkward moment when he selected me as the other half of an impromptu gag scene. To his great surprise, I answered him back and got a big laugh for myself. When the show was over, and he had taken numerous calls, he stopped me on the stage. 'Clever little girl,' was the comment, 'we'll do that again tomorrow. Come up to my room when you're dressed and we'll have a little drink and a little rehearsal.'

I was naturally elated, but the other girls laughed and more than hinted that I was wanted for something very different from a business chat.

However, he began in a business-like manner enough, complimented me on the way I had made his gag go, and in his quiet, incisive, clever way, suggested the necessary outlines of the working up.

Then he asked me to sit down, gave me a whisky and soda, and I noticed that his eye was devouring my charms with a hungry gleam. He began to let his conversation get rather frisky, and then boldy praised various portions of my body, my legs, my waist, and my breasts even. I finished my drink quickly and got up to go, but as I rose he followed me and clasped me in his arms before I had moved a step. I felt a passionate kiss on my throat, and his hand pressed roughly against the lower part of my stomach. I protested and struggled for I had no wish to make myself cheap in his eyes by an easy surrender. However, nothing was of any avail. He did not prolong the struggle, but calmly locked the door and proceeded to talk the matter over.

His arguments were pretty matter of fact. He was altogether carried away by my beauty he said, and was mad to enjoy me. What harm would be done? he argued, and he added that he could be a very good friend to me.

Of course, in the end I surrendered, and then came a very improper piece of business. Restall's costume necessitated skin tights, without any trunks, and, in case of any untoward swelling, he had his penis bound down to his stomach. So, when he had slipped off his tights, this curious arrangement met my astonished eyes – and he made me undo the wrapping till a fine stalwart member sprang from its bounds. I was surprised at its size, and condition, for Restall was a man of over fifty who had lived every day of his life. His position had brought him into contact with thousands of girls who were only too ready to submit to overtures, and, if rumour was to be trusted, he had availed himself of every opportunity. Also he was a drunkard; I don't suppose he had gone to bed sober any night for the last twenty-five years.

When once we got to business I was randy enough. There was no sofa, and the floor looked rather dirty, so he had me straddle-wise across his knees, forcing me down on to him till I had his penis within me right up to its hairy hilt. He grabbed me frightfully tight to him and fucked me quite brutally, but there was something in his savagery which delighted me. When it was over he drained a tremendously stiff whisky and soda and then sat back in the only big chair in the room. 'Well, you'd better be back to your room,' he said after a minute, 'the girls will be suspicious.'

'I thought as much,' I answered rather angrily, 'You've had all you want from me, and want to get rid of me.'

He became quite tender on the instant, and assured me that he meant nothing of the kind, only was nervous lest I should be suspected of over-familiarity with him. In fact he became so tenderly solicitous that he took me in his arms and kissed me – became naughty again, and the dirty beast fucked me again.

Nothing much of great interest happened during our three days' stay at Oxford – we were only allowed half a week by the University authorities, in accordance with the wise regulation that more than three days of the society of any particular set of musical comedy sirens is bad for the peace of mind of the undergraduates. I went out to all meals, some with my lordling, and some with the friends of Miss Sarel, the leading lady, who had graciously deigned to take me up. She was a bright, pretty little thing, quite passably clever, of a naughty temperament, and very much on the make as the theatrical saying goes; she came out of Oxford with one or two valuable presents in the jewellery line.

I was always stared at in the street, but the stare was not the sensual glance of the man about town who feels his cock raised at the appearance of an attractive female, but the simple admiration of a healthy young mind. Not that everything of a sensual nature was absent from our little stay, to say nothing of that already recounted scene in Restall's dressing room, for I experienced the beginning of a love affair.

One night the Sisters Knock brought home the tenor of the company to supper. Jean Messel was a strikingly handsome man, about thirty-five or so, I supposed, whose dark features betrayed a foreign origin. He had often eyed me at the theatre, but we had never spoken till this party. On this occasion, however, he found courage to press my hand, and, later, to snatch a kiss. That kiss set me on fire. I had known well enough before, the delights of a sensual feeling, but never a sensual feeling coupled with love. I dreamed of him all night, and the next morning when we met at the station, and exchanged some commonplace greeting, I experienced the sensation known as blushing all over, and was almost too timid to speak.

I did not continue in lodgings with Sisters Knock. Some little unpleasantness over my intimacy with the young Lord had arisen, to say nothing of my obvious attraction for Jean Messel; so at our next stop, which was Manchester, I chummed with a Miss Letty Ross, who played third principal part. Miss Ross had many acquaintances among the wealthy manufacturers of the north, fat, jolly, middle-aged men, with any amount of money, which they enjoyed spending, and a great deal of it which found its way into the pockets of the pretty little tarts of the various wandering companies. They wanted very little for their money, and I was glad of it, for my passion for the tenor produced a longing in my heart to remain quite chaste. Still one cannot exactly accept a diamond bangle for nothing, and more than once little Blanche suffered herself to be extended on the sofa of a hotel private room, and her dainty clothes elevated till the exposure of her naked charms caused some great Lancashire cock to crow lustily with anticipation. How hard they fucked, those north country merchants, and what quantities of sperm they spent, but they spent quantities of money, too, bless their enlarged hearts. At that time I grew very frightened of getting in the family way; those lusty devils were just the sort of men to get me caught, and I could not help a reciprocal spend when they came. However, Letty gave me some pills to take before my courses became due, and I escaped.

At Edinburgh, we boldly went to one of the best hotels, trusting to our fortune to find a mug to settle our bills, and sure enough we did find one, in the guise of a well known whisky distiller. He was staying in the same hotel and took on the two of us, first Letty and then myself. I was not jealous, for it gave me a rest, and I was really sweet to him on my nights. He swore his cock had never, never felt such pleasure. He was nearly sixty, but he had never been sucked off, so I cleaned his cock up one night, and taught him that. He nearly went off his head with joy.

On the Saturday night after an uncommonly good supper, and too many liqueurs, the old man falteringly asked if we two would mind his coming to bed with both of us. He had done so well during the week that we had not the heart to say no. We arranged for him to come to our bedroom in half an hour, when we should be undressed, but our door was barely closed behind us when in he slipped blushing like a schoolboy detected in a fault, and begging that he might be allowed to undress us himself.

He went for me first; I was wearing a three-quarter length frock that night, and the dear old gentleman got excited over it. I didn't raise a hand to help him myself, and he stripped me right to the buff. After he got me out of my bodice, and the skirt, his frenzied cock was nearly bursting his trousers, and when he had got me down to my drawers and vest, the poor panting things had to be released. I gave it just one pat with my hand and the spend flew all over me, covering my body right up to my neck, some of it even struck me in the face. He was disconsolate, and Letty was angry, said it was unfair to start so soon.

But Blanche was equal to the occasion. I sponged my face clean, did the same to his cock, told Letty to tongue his mouth, and we very soon had him stiff. Then he finished my undressing, till I sat in all my naked beauty on the bed before him. He was so randy again that he would have liked to fuck me again, then and there, but Letty naturally interfered. There was such a beautiful fire in the room that we both lay naked on the bed while our old friend tore off his clothes as if he was undressing for a swimming race against time.

Funnily enough though I often slept with Letty, not till that moment had I the least physical desire for her, but the filthiness of the whole scene overpowered me. I rolled over on top of her, feverishly fingered her pretty body and covered her lips with hot kisses which she returned in no half-hearted spirit. In a trice I had a finger up her cunt, so that ingress was barred to the old man. Next moment, however he was up me from behind, his arms gripping both our bodies, and he came in me while my lips were glued to Letty's and all my lust was for her. Still he must have had a good fuck, for I was wriggling my stomach against hers like fury. Even when he had finished I was so filthily randy that I drew my finger, all covered with spend from Letty's cunt and made him lick it clean, an innovation in sin which he thoroughly enjoyed.

Subsequently he fucked Letty and myself once more and that finished him. He shambled back to his bedroom, while Letty and I, after a hot bath together had one delicious bout of mutual cunt sucking, and then fell asleep in each other's arms.

Next morning when the bill was presented, our old friend had something of a shock, but he could not, after the events of the previous night, make any complaint.

I fancy that one hundred and two whiskies and sodas worried him. Of course, we didn't give it away that we had had all our friends in during the day time, while he was at his business, and he thoroughly believed we had slipped all that intolerable deal of liquor down our own fairy throats. He paid us the compliment of remarking that there wasn't a bonnie lassie from Maidenkirk to John of Groats could have done the like.

All this time I barely had an opportunity of seeing my dark-eyed Jean Messel. His wife, who figured in the bills as Miss Henden, became suspicious and never let him out her sight. She wasn't a bad little woman, and on the stage she looked very nice, but what a fake. To begin with, she wore lifters to give her an added inch in height. Then she wore low cut shoes displaying a nice curved pad where her instep should have been. When she went on the stage her legs were entirely encased in shapes, and even in ordinary walking dress, she sported hip pads. As for her bust, well, one night I got wet coming to the theatre and wanted a change of stockings. I found that every available stocking that woman had stuffed into her bodice. She even padded her arms, for she wore tightly-fitting transparent sleeves, and the flesh-coloured pads, that showed through had the appearance of the most fascinating rounded arms. Her neck and shoulders she enamelled. She wore yards of false hair, and what she had of her own was dyed. Her teeth, I need scarcely add, were removable at desire. Some of the girls used to question whether she had a false cunt or not.

One night Jean and I got a chance of a walk home from the theatre together, while she was at home ill. We came by a short cut through a mean street, lit only by an occasional lamp and towered over my gaunt, stark walls. We were quite alone, for it was late and very dark, and the neighbourhood had a dangerous reputation. There was no noise, save a faint flip-flop of water and presently we came to a place where the river was lazily licking a flight of stone steps. It was an eerie place, and I started nervously, brushing my shoulder against my companion. The next moment his arms were gripping me to him, and my lips sought his. I was willing enough to have let him have me, there and then, but presently he pushed me from him.

'Little Darling,' he said, 'next week my wife will not be with us. Shall we live in the same house?'

I said 'Yes,' with a kiss; and he saw me to my hotel door, and we parted.

Two Flappers in Paris

1

CROSSING THE CHANNEL

Without in any way disclosing my personality – which indeed, would be of no special interest to the reader – I may say that I occupy a somewhat important position in our Diplomatic Service, and it was in this capacity that I had to visit Paris in the month of October 19 . . .

I have often had occasion to visit Paris and it is always with the greatest pleasure that I return to this delightful city where every man can satisfy his tastes and desires whatever they may be. But on this occasion, more than ever before, chance, that great disposer of events, was to be on my side and had in store for me an adventure of the most delightful description.

I had had a pleasant run down to Folkestone and had gone on board one of those excellent boats which cross to Boulogne in something under two hours. It was blowing decidedly hard and the boat was rolling heavily but I did not mind this for I am a good sailor and I thought to myself that I should be able to enjoy in comparative solitude that delightful poetic feeling which results from a contemplation of the immensity of the ocean and of our own littleness as well as the wild beauty of a troubled sea.

And, as a matter of fact, the deck soon became deserted and I was left alone, but for the presence of a young girl who was standing by the side of the boat not far from me. From time to time my looks wandered from the white-crested waves and rested upon the charming figure that was before me, and finally I abandoned all contemplation of the infinite and all poetical and philosophical meditation and became wholly absorbed in my pretty travelling companion. For she was indeed lovely and the mobile and intellectual features of her charming face seemed to denote a very decided 'character.'

For a long time I admired her from a distance, but at last, by no means satisfied with this, I decided to try to make her acquaintance, and for this purpose I gradually approached her. At first she did not seem to notice me. Wearing, over her dress, a light waterproof which the strong wind wrapped closely round her body, she was leaning on her elbows on the rail, one hand placed under her chin and the other held the brim of her hat which otherwise would have stood a good chance of being carried away into the sea. She seemed to me to be about sixteen years old, but at the same time she was remarkably well made for a girl of that age. My eyes devoured the small and supple outline of her waist and the fine development of her behind which, placed as she was, she seemed to be offering to some bold caress, unless perchance it might be to a still more delightful punishment . . .

On her feet she wore a charming pair of high-heeled brown shoes which set off to the best advantage the smallness and daintiness of her extremities.

I came close up to her without her making the slightest movement or even looking in my direction, and I stood for a few moments without saying a word, taking a subtle and intimate pleasure in examining every detail of her beauty; her splendid thick pig-tail of dark silky hair, the fine arch of her ears, the whiteness of her neck, the near delicacy of her eyebrows, and what I could see of her splendid dark eyes, the aristocratic smallness of her nose and its mobile nostrils, the softness of her rosy little mouth and the animation of her healthy complexion.

Then suddenly I made up my mind.

'We are in for a rough crossing!' I said. She turned slowly towards me her little head and for a moment examined me in silence. And now, seen full face, I found her even more beautiful and more attractive than she had seemed before when I had only been able to obtain a side view of her.

Apparently her examination of me was favourable, for a slight smile disclosed the prettiest little teeth that it was possible to imagine and she answered.

'Do you think so? I don't mind if we are!' this paradoxical answer was quite in keeping with her appearance.

'I congratulate you.' I said, 'I see that you are a true English girl, and that a rough sea has no terrors for you!'

'Oh,' said she quickly, 'I'm not afraid of anything; and as for the sea, I love it. Of all amusements I like yachting best.' I could not help laughing a little. Evidently of all the amusements that she was acquainted with yachting might be her favourite one, but a day would come, and perhaps was not far off, when she would know others: and then, yachting . . .

However, I considered that it was impossible to continue the conversation without having gained her confidence, and to effect this my best plan was to introduce myself.

'You must excuse me,' I said, 'for having taken the liberty of speaking to you, but our presence on the deck here, when everybody else has taken refuge below, seems to indicate that we are intended to know one another . . . and, I hope, to appreciate one another. My name is Jack W—, and I am attached to our Foreign Office.'

She gave me a charming little bow, and, at once, by the smile in her eyes I could see that I had attained my object.

'And my name,' said she, 'is Evelyn H . . . and I am on my way to school. I am travelling alone as far as Boulogne but there a French governess will meet me and take me on to Paris.'

Let me here state that I cannot mention her surname nor that of any of the other characters who will appear in this story, which is an absolutely true one in every particular, for some of the characters are well known in society and might be known to some of my readers.

'Oh really?' I exclaimed. 'You are on your way to Paris? I'm going there too. What bad luck that we can't travel all the way together. But at any rate we can keep one another company till we reach Boulogne. Shall we sit down together in that shelter: we shall be fairly out of the wind there?'

There was a convenient seat close by which we proceeded to occupy. My blood was already beginning to course more freely through my veins.

'Where are you going to in Paris?'

'To Mme X . . . at Neuilly. That's where I am at school.'

'I know the school well,' said I. 'It is certainly the most fashionable one in all Paris. I suppose there are a large number of girls there?'

'No, not more than sixty.'

'You are one of the elder girls?'

'No, not yet!' said she, uttering a sigh. 'I wish I were, but I shall have to wait till next year for that.'

'And why are you so anxious to be one of the elder girls?'

She gave me a rapid glance and smiled.

'Because,' said she, 'the elder girls know things that we don't know . . .'

'What sort of things?'

'Oh, all sorts of things. And they are very proud of their superior knowledge let me tell you.

They say that we are too young to join their Society.'

'And what is this Society?'

'It's a secret Society. They call it, I don't know why, the *Lesbian Society*. But after all what does it matter: our time will come!'

I was more and more delighted with Evelyn's candour and with the decidedly interesting turn which our conversation had taken.

'Oh, yes. I have a special friend there who is more than a sister to me. We have no secrets from one another. Her name is Nora A . . . and I love the walks we have together.'

'You go into Paris sometimes, I suppose?'

'Yes, but of course there is always some one with us to chaperone us.'

'Have you ever been to the Louvre?'

'Oh, yes! What beautiful pictures, and other things too, that are there.'

'The statues for instance; you have seen them? Now tell me, were you not rather surprised when you saw the statues of the men without any fig leaves as they are always represented with in our galleries?'

Evelyn blushed slightly and smiled. I saw her eyes sparkle but she covered them with her long lashes.

'At first I was,' said she. 'And of course I noticed the difference that there is between . . .'

She stopped and nervously began to tap her knees.

'Between what?' I said. 'Between a man and a woman?'

126

'Yes . . .'

'The statues,' I continued, 'do not give you a very exact idea of the difference. I have often said to myself, when I have watched a bevy of our charming school-girls in the statue room examining the statues, that this difference would be much more pronounced and obvious if the statues of the men were real men, and if these men knew that they were the objects of admiration of a number of pretty girls!'

Evelyn raised her eyes to mine filled with a kind of mute interrogation.

'I don't understand what you mean,' said she after a short pause.

I hesitated for a moment but only for a moment. Already I was plunging headlong into this delightful adventure the memory of which, in its minutest details, will never leave me.

'You don't understand?' I resumed, moving a little closer to her so that now our forms were actually in contact, and taking her little hand which she abandoned to me with a slight tremble of emotion. 'I will explain it to you. It's quite simple and these are things that a girl must know some time or other; and, upon my word, in my opinion the sooner they know them the better.' Her little hand seemed fairly to burn mine and her lovely eyes, full of curiosity gazed into mine and I felt that already a powerful tie existed between us. How completely I had forgotten the magnificent surroundings of sky and sea!

'You must have noticed that the statues of the

men,' I observed, 'are not like those of the women?'

'Oh, yes, of course,' said she and her colour deepened. 'The forms are different.'

'Yes, the breasts of women are much more developed, their waists are smaller, their hips broader and fuller, the seat is much longer and plumper, and the thighs are bigger and rounder. But there is something else too – ! You know what I mean'

'Yes,' she murmered.

A troubled look seemed to fill her eyes.

'And this something else,' I continued, 'did you notice how it was made?'

'I . . . yes . . . I think I noticed it . . .'

'It's like a great fruit, as large as a peach, with a double kernel, isn't it? And hanging down over is a kind of appendage: it is like a rolled up loaf of flesh which seems to wish to hide the fruit . . .'

'Oh, yes, it's just like that!'

'That is the way that sculptors represent what is called "the male sex." But as a matter of fact it is not really made like that, at least not the appendage. This object which you have seen hanging down and lifeless is, in reality, the most sensitive, the most lively, and the most change-able thing that it is possible to imagine. It is the most wonderful thing that exists and also the most precious, for it is capable of giving life and the most delightful pleasure.'

Evelyn was evidently much excited but her eyes avoided mine as she murmured.

'I think I understand . . . It is with that . . . that babies are made.'

'Exactly!'

'Then,' she continued almost in a whisper, 'each time that . . . that a man makes use of that thing is . . . is a baby made?'

The laugh with which this innocent question provoked in me completed Evelyn's confusion. She hid her lovely face, now blushing crimson, in her hands. I whispered in her ear.

'Forgive me for laughing, but your innocence is perfectly charming. But how is it that you know so little about such things? Have your companions at school never told you about anything?'

'No,' said she. 'I am only seventeen and a half, and I shall not be able to join the Society which I have mentioned to you till I am eighteen.'

'Tell me more about this Society.'

'The elder girls call it the "Lesbian Society." I just long to be a member of it, as, indeed, do all the girls who are not yet seventeen. Oh, what jokes they must have together and what things they must do! If only, before joining the Society, I could know as much as the "seniors." What a score it would be, and how delighted I should be!'

'Oh,' said I, 'there's no difficulty about that. You need only have complete confidence in me, and to let me act as your instructor. It would be a great pleasure to me and a real advantage to yourself. And, in the first place, let me tell you that you have nothing to fear from me, nor from anyone else while I am looking after you. Now, tell me, have you ever seen any naughty photos or cinema films?'

She shook her pretty head.

'No,' said she, 'but how I should love to see some.'

'Well, that could easily be managed, and you would see then how one can make use of what we were talking about just now without there being the slightest fear of a baby resulting! And this information I consider not only useful but absolutely necessary for a well-brought-up young lady.'

I must confess that so much candour, combined with such charming grace, excited me strangely. I took her soft delicate hand which she abandoned to me readily and continued.

'As we are both going to Paris, and as Paris above all other places lends itself to obtaining instruction in all matters in which you are so interested, we must arrange some plan which will, I think, be as simple as it will be certain . . .'

'Oh, do go on!' said Evelyn.

'Well, this is my idea. When we are settled, you at your school, and I at the British Embassy, I will write to you, pretending to be your uncle, and will offer to take you out for the afternoon. My letter, written on the official Embassy note paper, will, I feel sure, have the desired effect and will readily induce your head-mistress to let you come out with me. What do you think of my scheme?'

'It's splendid! but there's one thing I must tell

you. Madame has a rule that no girl is ever allowed to go out alone with a gentleman, even if he is a near relation . . .'

'What on earth is to be done then?'

'Wait a moment! If, however, the gentleman invites another girl to accompany his relation, then Madame never raises any objection.'

'Ah, really!' I said, feeling somewhat disappointed, for I did not care for this idea of a second girl, which might upset my plans.

'So, if you would invite Nora,' continued Evelyn calmly, 'the matter would go swimmingly, I'm certain.'

'Nora, and who may she be?'

'My friend, the girl I was telling you about. Oh, she's perfectly charming and would be so delighted to know about . . . about things!'

'Right you are then; by all means let Nora come too. You are sure we can trust her?'

'Absolutely certain.'

'She is a real friend? She has your tastes? She thoroughly understands you?'

'Nora is more than a sister to me. She seems to guess my thoughts almost before I have formed them: and then, if I am seedy, nobody knows how to comfort me as she does. Oh, her kisses are delightful; and sometimes she bathes me in her beautiful golden hair which is much finer than mine, and mine is generally considered rather nice. But the chief charm about her is sweet manners, sometimes serious but more often roguish. Oh, you have no idea what a little darling she is!'

131

'Little?'

'Oh, that's only a way of speaking. She is about as tall as I am and rather bigger, and so chic and has such a beautiful figure, and she dresses delightfully, almost like a "Parisienne". But you will see! Oh, what splendid fun we three will have together; you see if we don't . . . uncle!'

'Your uncle, Evelyn – you must let me call you by your Christian name – is delighted to have discovered a niece at once so fresh, so beautiful, so sensible, and so eager for information. He undertakes to make you easily surpass in knowledge all the young ladies in the Lesbian Society, so that, when your age permits you to join the secret circles of this mysterious club, you will astonish your fellow members by your remarkable knowledge of matters which are always of the greatest interest to girls!'

And so we chatted on till the boat was about to enter the harbour of Boulogne where we parted with much mutual regret, lest the governess who had come to meet Evelyn should see us together. Short as had been our acquaintance we had indeed become good friends.

2

A HIGH CLASS 'MAISON CLOSE'

That same afternoon, having no official business to attend to till the following morning, I made my way to the most famous of all Parisian 'bordels', that kept by Madame R in the rue Ch—. I had made up my mind to put my plan into operation as quickly as possible, for I was afraid that Evelyn might, either of her own accord, or after consultation with Nora, change her mind.

'La donna e mobile! . . .' as says the old song.

I was shown into the private boudoir of the good lady of the house whom I had known well for some years, and I am in no way boasting when I say that I was received with open arms both by her and my little acquaintance, Rose, the prettiest, gayest and most attractive inmate of the whole house, who knew me, and used to introduce me to her friends, by the name 'Monsieur Quatrefois', because, excited by her charms, I had acomplished with her four times in little more than one hour what many husbands take four weeks to achieve with their wives. Rose had been educated at a good school in England and spoke our language better than almost any other foreigner that I have ever met. She used always to prefer speaking English with me though I am a good French scholar and enjoy conversing in that musical and prolific language that gives a soul to the objects of sense and a body to the abstractions of philosophy.

When I had satisfied the insatiable curiosity of Rose and answered her numerous questions, I proceeded to explain to Madame R the main object of my visit.

'My dear lady,' I said, 'I have had the most extraordinary piece of good fortune. I have made the acquaintance of two young maidens, two little flappers who are absolutely fresh and innocent, and I have promised to bring them to your house and to let them see some of your interesting cinema films.' I then explained to Madame what had happened on the boat. At first she raised loud objections, the adventure seemed to her altogether too risky, but after further discussion, and influenced no doubt by the liberal terms I offered, she began to change her tone and finally agreed to assist in the carrying out of my plan, laying down however one condition as indispensable, that the maiden heads of the young ladies should not be tampered with. This she considered necessary in view of possible subsequent troubles; as for anything else, to use her own strong expression, 'elle s'en battait l'oeil,' which being interpreted means that she didn't care a fig. This having been agreed to we proceeded to arrange the programme of the little entertainment which I was organising for my two little novices and . . . for myself.

In the first place it was settled that we should visit the cinema room, where should be displayed to us one of the most interesting films of Madame's collection, 'The Devil in Hell' of Boccaccio. The picture could be repeated so that they might become thoroughly acquainted with every detail.

Then we were to visit the drawing-room and the ladies of the house would be presented to us. I knew them all and how carefully and well they had been trained by Madame, and as nothing is more like a real lady than a stylish demi-mondaine I was certain that nothing would be done to shock my two flappers. Anything that the girls of the house might do, in connivance with me, would seem to them some mysterious rite, at last disclosed to their ardent curiosity, and which they would be most interested to watch.

Next taking Rose with us, to act as instructor in certain particulars, we were to first visit the Spanking Room, and then the room of the Armchair of Pleasure.

In each of these rooms Rose and I would explain by word and action the use of the room, and of the instrument and furniture to be found there: and as I thought over this part of the programme I entertained the hope that Evelyn and Nora might themselves be induced to experience the sensations which Rose and I were describing to them.

I left the house, this time without having paid my homage to the charms of Rose who, like a thoughtful girl, advised me to keep all my powers in reserve as, when I visited the establishment with my little friends, they would certainly be taxed to the utmost. Early the next morning I made my way from the Hotel Meurice, where I had put up, to the English Embassy and transacted the most pressing part of the business which had brought me to Paris. I took advantage of being there to write a note to Evelyn on the official notepaper offering to take her out with me that same afternoon, and saying that I should be glad to see one of her companions with her if she cared to bring one. I signed myself Uncle Jack, and gave the address of my hotel. I then despatched the note by a special messenger.

By mid-day I received a wire in reply at my hotel from my 'niece' informing me that she would be delighted to be taken out and that she would be accompanied by her friend Nora.

I could not help rubbing my hands with pleasure. Events were proceeding just as Evelyn and I had anticipated. The gods were evidently on our side!

I at once secured a taxi and set out for the school where I was most cordially received by Madame X. She apologised for having to put in force her rule with regard to not allowing any one of her girls to go out alone with a gentleman, and informed me that her two young pupils were dressing and would be ready almost immediately.

In a few moments they appeared, delightfully dressed and quite rosy with emotion at the idea of this outing which, as Evelyn said, was all the more welcome as it was so entirely unexpected.

I thought it was decidely unwise to prolong the interview with Madame who might easily have asked some awkward questions, so said that we would start at once. I directed my chauffeur to drive us to the Café Americain.

It was a lovely day, such as one often has in Paris in the month of October. The terrace of the famous café was crowded with people but we managed to find three seats and at once I could not fail to notice that the beauty, the grace, the youth, and the charming get-up of my two companions attracted the eyes of all who were present.

And this admiration was indeed well deserved. I have already given a description of Evelyn. I have noted her beautiful dark eyes and hair, the delicacy of her features, ease and elegance of her carriage, and the aristocratic smallness of her hands and feet.

She was wearing a charming crêpe de Chine frock of light pink colour, with a broad crimson sash round her waist, and a pretty bow of the same material at the end of her splendid pig-tail. The blouse, which had a small sailor collar, and the fronts and pocket of which were ornamented with hemstitching, was decidedly open in front thus allowing a glimpse to be obtained of her lovely budding breasts. A sailor hat, in silk beaver, with folded crown, and finished with silk Petersham set off the beauty of her hair and eyes to perfection. The skirt was just pleasantly short, thus allowing one to see the beginning of a beautifully shaped pair of legs which were encased in open-work black silk stockings, the feet being shod in a dainty pair of high-heeled French shoes.

Nora, as I have said, was fair: of that delightful fairness which one so often comes across in the North of Ireland. Her eyes were a lovely deep blue, her nose small, her nostrils palpitating and sensual, while a rosy-lipped little mouth permitted one to see two perfect rows of pearly-white teeth. Such were the chief features of Nora's really lovely face. Do not, however, let it be supposed for a moment that she was in the least doll-like! Far from it! She was remarkably lively and gay, and had a most winning and attractive smile, and as I think of her I recall to myself the opening words of the old song of Tralee:

'She was lovely and fair like the roses in midsummer, yet 'twas not her beauty all alone that won me!'

She was wearing a pretty dress of light blue cotton voile, with a blue sash to match and a blue ribbon at the end of her pig-tail, which I noticed was even longer and thicker than Evelyn's, as the latter had told me. Light blue stockings, a pair of high-heeled brown shoes, and a becoming straw hat completed a most charming costume such as you may see so often on 'Children's Day'

138

at Ranelagh, or at Lords on the day of the Eton and Harrow match.

We did not stay long on the terrace but mounted to the restaurant on the first floor, the girls being much amused at the number of mirrors that decorated the stair-case. There we enjoyed a most excellent lunch and consumed between us a bottle and a half of champagne.

Evelyn and Nora had become quite merry and their colour had risen, so I thought that the time had now come to speak of what, no doubt, was in the minds of us all.

'Now, tell me, Evelyn,' I said, 'does your friend know about our conversation on the boat?'

'Oh!' said Evelyn laughing a little nervously, 'if she didn't she wouldn't be here!'

Nora blushed deeply but began to laugh too.

'Capital!' said I. 'Now tell me frankly. Are you both prepared to pass a decidedly . . . unconventional afternoon?'

The two girls were now equally red and they were none the less charming for that.

'We are prepared for anything!' said Evelyn.

'Is that correct, Nora?'

'Quite correct!' said Nora after a moment's hesitation.

'And the more . . . "unconventional" the better,' said Evelyn, hiding her face behind one of the little fans which I had just handed to her.

'That's right,' said I. 'Now we must come to certain arrangements. Nora, like you, must call me "Uncle Jack": You are my two nieces, do you understand?'

'Oh, yes, yes!'

'And next, you must not be surprised at anything, but must have complete confidence in me. I can promise you one thing: that you will come through all the experiences that we are about to encounter as intact, physically I mean, as you are at the present moment. You understand what I mean?'

Both of them seemed to tremble a little, but after a quick glance at one another Evelyn answered:

'Yes, we understand, and that's just what we should have wished.'

'Capital!'

'There's only one thing that we are anxious about,' said Nora, who was becoming more and more at her ease with me; 'and that is to know more than the girls of the Lesbian Society, and to be able to . . . to . . . what do the French say? a funny word . . .'

'To "epater" them?' I asked.

'Yes, that's it! To "epater" them.'

'Very well, my dear nieces! I will guarantee that you shall be able to fairly "epater" them if you relate faithfully to them all that you are going to see and learn this afternoon. And now we ought to be on the move.'

I settled the bill and sending for a taxi, very pleased with ourselves, we set off for the rue Ch—.

3

THE DEVIL IN HELL

As had been arranged we were received by Madame R who showed us into her private sitting-room. There was nothing to give a hint to my 'nieces' as to the occupation of the lady of the house, and accordingly they were very curious as to who and what she might be. Madame R having left us alone for a few moments to attend to the details of the arrangements. Evelyn and Nora began eagerly to question me.

'Where are we? Who is the lady? Dear Uncle Jack, do tell us: oh, please do!'

The champagne assisting, they became so pressing that I felt my own feelings beginning to rise. The contact with this young and charming pair, the idea of their absolute virginity in which wholly unknown sensations were so soon to be aroused, their eager and warm looks, the pressure of their hot and soft little hands, all this seemed to endow me with all my youthful vigour, and I felt standing up inside my trousers the delicate and sensitive instrument of flesh, by which man measures in himself the degree of his sensual pleasure, as hard and stiff as it would have been had I knocked off fifteen of my thirty-five years.

'My dear children,' said I, 'restrain yourselves. I am here only to instruct and, I hope, amuse you. The house belongs to a lady friend of mine. She is the manageress of a Temple to which one can come to adore, in return for a liberal remuneration, the goddess of Pleasure!'

'Oh, Uncle Jack, how you do tease!' said Evelyn with a delightful little pout. 'Do put things more plainly!'

'Very well then! There are certain houses where men, by paying liberally, can enjoy all the pleasures of the senses. In these houses . . .'

'Then,' broke in Nora eagerly, 'it is this lady who provides these pleasures?'

I began to laugh.

'Not exactly the lady herself,' I said. 'She has some assistants, charming girls and young women, who have not taken a vow of chastity, who are no longer virgins, and who make themselves agreeable to gentlemen who are nice to them and pay them well.'

'Oh, I never! . . .' broke in Evelyn with astonishment. 'How can they? For my part I shall love one man . . . perhaps two, but not a whole lot!'

'That's right,' I said. 'You are very sensible, Evelyn; but these girls are sensible and practical too. They know what you are ignorant of at present but have come here to learn. Thanks to their instructions you will presently be more learned, not only than all your companions of the

Lesbian Society, but also than most ladies even if they have been married for twenty years and to a husband who lets himself go in his marital relations!'

Evelyn clapped her hands with pleasure, but Nora, who had got up from her chair, and was making an inspection of the room, called out to us and beckoned us to approach.

She was examining a fine 18th century engraving which bore this delightful title 'The Whipping of Cupid.'

The artist had represented the chubby, well-developed lad half-lying across the divine knees of his mother, Venus, who, with a bunch of roses instead of a rod, was applying to his bottom the charming punishment.

The two girls examined the picture, blushing scarlet.

'This is symbolical,' I said. 'Love is often whipped!'

'Oh,' said Evelyn, 'but why?'

'Well, you will know later on! The birch, nicely applied by a skilful hand, is the most delightful caress, don't forget that! But I hear steps, let us sit down again.'

Scarcely had we resumed our seats when the door opened and Madame R appeared.

'If you will be so good as to follow me,' she said, 'I will show you the cinema room, I have arranged a little entertainment for you.'

We got up and followed her.

The room was small but comfortably furnished. Facing the stage, or rather the sheet, were five boxes the partitions of which nearly reached to the ceiling. In the one that we entered were three chairs and behind them, a small sofa. We took our places on the chairs, I of course sitting in the centre, and Madame left us, saying as she retired:

'If you require me touch the bell, and I will be with you in a moment.'

Then we were left alone.

Suddenly words appeared on the sheet and we read.

> Before the representation of
> 'The Devil in Hell.'
> We present a slight sketch.
> 'Miss Barbara, school-mistress.'

And at once this first film, which I had not been expecting, was set in motion.

The picture represented a class-room fitted up in the usual way with a teacher's desk, blackboard, maps and pupil's desks, etc. One of these desks was occupied by a nice looking, well-made young man. At first he was writing but suddenly he rose from his place and made for the teacher's desk where he immediately proceeded to upset the ink-stand; he then went to the blackboard and, with a piece of chalk, drew a ludicrous head of a woman with a huge chignon and large goggle eye-glasses. Having done this he resumed his seat and a moment later the door opened and Miss Barbara, school-mistress, sailed into the room. She was a fine young woman of about thirty with a learned and severe expression. She soon discovered the condition of her desk and the drawing on the blackboard. Examining the lad's fingers she found direct evidence that he was the culprit.

An inscription appeared on the sheet.

'So you have been up to your tricks again, Billy. Very well, sir. I shall have to give you another whipping. Prepare yourself!'

She came up to Billy and took him by the hand; then she drew him towards the open part of the room, that is to say towards the spectators, and having removed his coat proceeded to unbutton and let down his trousers. Having slipped them down to his knees, she tucked his shirt in under his waistcoat both behind and in front thus completely exposing the boy from the waist to the knees. She then, with her left arm, bent him over and with her right hand began to smack his bottom soundly. It was a most amusing sight to see the youth wriggle and dance under the smarting whipping that he was receiving but what raised the emotion of my two little friends to the highest point was the sight of Billy's tool in a full state of erection which could be plainly seen when, in his struggles, he was turned towards us.

Both of the girls had seized one of my hands and were squeezing it hard. I could feel that they were highly excited and all their nerves were on the stretch, and Evelyn whispered to me:

'It's not a bit like it is on the statues now! . . .'

Miss Barbara paused in her whipping and seemed to become aware, with a well-feigned indignation, of Billy's disgracefully indecent condition.

First she pointed with apparent horror at the

offending instrument, then she took it in her hand and began to move the soft skin up and down, and then the film, changing suddenly, showed only the hand, very much enlarged, working the skin up and down, and covering and uncovering the well-defined head.

Evelyn and Nora, as the picture changed, uttered a little cry and gripped my hands still more tightly, and Nora asked me softly:

'Is she punishing him in doing that, Uncle Jack?'

'It is a punishment which is really a caress,' I said, 'and it acts through the feeling of shame, and the effect which it has on Billy's modesty.'

'Oh!' sighed Evelyn, 'how I should love to punish a naughty lad like that!'

Her looks were bathed in voluptuousness and Nora was in the same condition.

'Yes,' said I, 'but you would have to spank him first.'

'So much the better! I should like to do that too!'

Then the film returned to its normal size and Miss Barbara began to smack her young pupil again, at the same time passing her left hand well round his waist and taking a firm hold of his well developed young prick. At last the punishment was over, Billy received his pardon with a warm kiss from his mistress, they left the room together, the film was cut off, and the light turned on in the room. . . . My two 'nieces' at the same moment heaved a great sigh of satisfaction.

'Well,' said I, 'did that interest you?'

'Oh! yes,' said Evelyn, and Nora agreed. 'I had never seen this . . . this thing in that condition. I had no idea that it was made like that. Was Miss Barbara hurting Billy when she rubbed his thing like that?'

'Certainly not,' I answered, 'quite the contrary! And I am quite certain that he would gladly have received another spanking on condition of being treated in the same way after it.' Nora, blushing delightfully murmered:

'Uncle Jack, shall we be able to see this . . . thing . . . really? A real live one, I mean?'

'If you are very good girls perhaps I shall be able to let you see a real live one! This thing as you call it is called a "prick" but you must never pronounce this word in public. You must not even speak of the thing. It is enough to know about it and to think about it. And now, you darlings, let me tell you that this thing is capable of giving girls the greatest pleasure that it is possible for them to experience.'

'Oh! I can quite believe that!' said Evelyn. 'How delightful it must be to touch it, to stroke it, and to fondle it as Miss Barbara was doing!'

'Quite right, Evelyn, but the pleasure which you would feel in doing that is not to be compared with the other, the true, the supreme pleasure, which results from the introduction and movements of the prick in . . . in . . .'

'In what, Uncle Jack?' asked Nora tenderly.

'In what corresponds in you girls to what we men have; you know what I mean! . . . Come now, don't you?'

'Oh,' sighed Evelyn, looking sweetly confused; 'do you mean in . . . in the little crack . . .'

'Just so, Evelyn. This little crack is the entrance to the sheath which nature has provided in woman to receive the "prick" of man.'

'Really?' sighed Nora. 'And is that how babies are made?'

'Yes, indeed it is, Nora. But one can enjoy pleasure, in fact the complete pleasure, without having children. One can even enjoy this supreme pleasure without being obliged to introduce the "prick" into the rosy little nest which you girls have ready for it, and you will know presently how this can be done. But I wanted you first of all to know the natural destination of this living sceptre which man always carries about with him, for you will understand better the film which is to follow and which is called "The Devil in Hell." The Devil is the "prick". The hell is the hot little nest towards which destiny urges him . . .'

'Oh!'

They uttered this 'oh!' both together. Their minds were being opened; they were now for the first time catching a glimpse of new worlds filled with strange and voluptuous marvels. I was intensely excited as can easily be imagined, and it was with difficulty that I restrained myself from at once proceeding to caress the two charming girls and from teaching them how to caress me. But I have always been a man of method, and having fixed on a plan I was determined to carry it out in every particular.

Discreet taps were heard at the door and in

reply to my call to come in Madame entered the room.

'And how did you like "Miss Barbara," ' she asked me.

'It was quite interesting,' I replied, 'but the end seemed rather tame.'

Madame laughed.

'The end is really quite different,' she said. 'The sketch was only intended as an introduction with the object of preparing the young ladies for the picture which will follow . . . I thought that you would explain it to them sufficiently and I did not wish in any way to detract from the effect of "The Devil in Hell" in which the incidents are much more exciting and given with much greater detail than in "Miss Barbara".'

'What then is the real ending of the film which we have just seen?'

'You saw Miss Barbara lead Billy away. She conducts him to her own room where she gives him a very complete lesson in the way in which a man should behave to a lady. And now I think you are ready for "The Devil in Hell", but would you not be more comfortable on this little sofa, see, there is just room for the three of you.'

I at once appreciated the excellence of Madame's advice, and moving the chairs and putting the sofa in their place we took our seat upon it; Madame then left us and the light was again turned off.

Instinctively Evelyn and Nora moved close up on each side of me. I took advantage of this to place my arm round their waist and then, gently and with infinite care, my hands slipped down and I began to stroke and fondle the outside of their thighs and of their soft young bottoms. It was most interesting to notice that neither of the girls raised the slightest objection to this little attention, but on the contrary each slightly raised the cheek that I was squeezing as though inviting my hand to pass more completely underneath!

Meanwhile the film began to be displayed.

I must describe it as shortly as possible, although for my own satisfaction and for that of my readers I should much like to dwell in detail on the voluptuous scenes which took place between the charming and naive little Alibech and the cunning hermit, Father Rustique.

In the first scene, which might have been a landscape from the 'Arabian Nights' we saw a lovely girl of about seventeen dressed in oriental costume, approach an old man. Headlines informed us that Alibech, a young girl of Caspia, was anxious to lead a religious life and was asking the old sage how this could be done.

'You must abandon pomps and vanities of this wicked world and live as the Christians do in the deserts of Thebais,' said the old man. Next we saw Alibech setting out for these famous deserts. She was very lightly clad, for the weather was very hot, and the glimpse which from time to time I caught of her lovely forms made me think that I would gladly play with her the part which was to be taken by the hermit.

Presently Alibech reached the hut of a lonely saint and explained to him her mission.

Astonished, but fearing, at the sight of her beauty, that the devil might tempt him, he praised her zeal but would not keep her; he however directed her to a holy man, who, as he said, was much more fitted to instruct her than himself.

She therefore goes on her way and soon arrives at the abode of Father Rustique, for such is the name of the saint in question. Like his good brother he questions her, and, relying on his moral strength, decides to keep her with him.

Father Rustique is a handsome young man in the prime of life and we soon see by his burning looks, his gestures and his attitudes that he is a prey to the demon of the flesh. He succumbs. But in order that the sin may be his alone he makes use of a stratagem to accomplish his ends.

He explains to the innocent girl that the great enemy of mankind is the devil and that the most meritorious act that a Christian can do is to put him as often as possible into the hell for which he is destined!

Alibech asks him how that is to be done.

'I will show you directly,' says Rustique, 'you have only to do as you see me do . . .' Then he begins to undress and the girl does the same. When they are completely naked he kneels down and placing the beautiful woman before him his eyes wander over the lovely charms which are now fully exposed to his enraptured gaze.

The girl looks timidly at the Father and suddenly her eyes are filled with astonishment and pointing to a great thing which is standing out from the holy man's belly she asks:

'What is that, which is quite unlike any thing that I have?'

'It is the devil,' says Rustique, 'which I have been telling you about. See how it torments me and how fierce and proud it is!'

'Ah, how thankful I ought to be that I have not such a devil, since it is so troublesome to you!'

'Yes,' says Rustique, 'but you have something else instead!'

'And what is that?'

'The hell!'

At this Alibech shows the greatest fear, and the Father goes on:

'And I think that you must have been sent here expressly for the salvation of my soul, for if the devil continues to torment me and if you will permit me to put him into your hell we shall be doing the most meritorious action that it is possible to do.'

Alibech states that she is quite willing to do whatever the holy Father may deem right.

He immediately takes the naked girl in his arms and, carrying her into the hut, places her on her back on the little couch, and opens her thighs as wide as possible. Then he kneels between them and for a few moments examines with gleaming eyes the lovely body exposed before him. Then stretching himself along the docile little virgin, and taking a firm hold on her, he whispers to her to take hold of the devil and guide him into hell.

The obedient young woman obeys and the head of the devil is placed in the very jaws of hell. With a downward thrust of his powerful bottom the Father begins his attack and the head of the devil enters the outskirts of his domains. A look of surprise comes over Alibech's face, and as, with another powerful thrust, the devil is driven half way home, and the obstacle which stood in his way is pierced, a little cry is drawn from her lips and is followed by another as, with another steady lunge, the devil is driven up to the hilt into his burning home. For a few moments the hermit lay enjoying the completeness of his victory. Then his bottom was set in motion and the devil was driven in and out . . . in and out . . . in and out, slowly at first and then quicker and quicker, till a spasm seemed to shake the whole of his body, and the convulsive jerks of his bottom showed that the devil was pouring out into hell the very vials of his wrath.

One bout however was not sufficient to humble the pride of satan and it was not till he had been plunged into hell on three separate occasions that his head finally drooped, when the hermit rested and allowed his little partner to repose also.

All this time I had been pressing Evelyn and Nora closely to me and from time to time I had taken a stealthy glance at them.

They had watched the development of the story panting with pleasure, their lips slightly open as though inviting my kisses, their eye-lids drooping, and their cheeks suffused with blushes. I could feel them quiver with the depth of emotion of young virgins before whom the mysteries of life are being unfolded.

Each time that Father Rustique buried his devil in hell, one could see, thanks to the excellent way in which the picture was presented, the great red head penetrate the fresh young lips, as pouting and soft as the mouth of a baby, and then work its way in and out, till the final spasm shook the lucky hermit. And all this time I could feel the two girls trembling with emotion, their bodies stiffened and contracted with the intensity of a desire hitherto wholly unknown to them.

And now the film was set in motion again, and we could see, on the next day, the holy Father recommence with his charming pupil his pious exercises. And now it was evident by her lascivious motions that Alibech was beginning to find these religious observances exceedingly pleasant, so that she was plainly urging the good hermit to be as zealous as possible in the prosecution of his good works; and as her imagination developed in the joy experienced in thus doing her pleasant duty she invented new positions and fresh ways of inserting the Father's devil into her hot little hell.

Thus it was that we saw her kneel on the edge of the bed and present her lovely soft bottom as if she had been inviting her companion to chastise her. But he knowing that this was not her intention, and excited by this delightful situation, opened the thighs of the little angel and plunged his weapon into her from behind. And here too every detail of the operation was most admirably represented. And so the picture went on and on and Alibech became more and more expert in varying the method of putting the devil into hell. Sometimes, so as not to fatigue her instructor, she would place him on a chair and then getting astride of him, so turning her back to us, she would, a thoughtful girl, take all the hard work on herself, and here too we could see that she made as excellent a rider as she had proved herself a docile mount.

Nora, who had very quickly become perfectly at her ease with me, while this little scene was in progress, pressed my hand which was squeezing her trembling bottom, and resting her sweet head against my shoulder, whispered in my ear:

'Oh! Uncle Jack, Uncle Jack!'

'You would like to be in Thebais, Nora, dear?' She only answered by an eloquent look, in which already the voluptuous and lovable woman which she was to become later on was revealed to me.

Evelyn said nothing but I was aware that she was just as excited as Nora. She did not miss a single point of the interesting entertainment which I had provided for her, and I felt sure that she was registering every detail in her faithful memory in order, later on, to be able to overwhelm with her science the 'seniors' of the Lesbian Society.

I will leave the reader to imagine the condition in which I was myself during all this time. I do not wish to dwell on this more than I can help, my object being, as far as possible, to write of these things *objectively* to use the expression of a certain modern school.

Then, as the picture went on, we saw the repeated punishment of the devil beginning to have its inevitable effect on the worthy hermit, whose food consisted for the most part only of fruit and water. Little Alibech became distressed at his want of zeal and found it necessary to rouse the devil into action, till at last, evidently much to her disappointment, Father Rustique had to inform her that his devil was now thoroughly humbled and would not trouble him for some little time.

The light having been turned on in the room, my two companions awoke from the voluptuous dream which they had been living through and sighed deeply.

'Oh!' said Evelyn, arching her delightfully supple and small waist. 'I should have liked it to go on forever!'

'Really?' said I: 'so it interested you very much?'

'Oh! yes. And you too, Nora, didn't it?'

'I should think it did,' said Nora. 'I can't imagine anything more delightful and exciting!'

'But what I can't understand,' said Evelyn excitedly, 'is how the devil which is so big can get into the hell which is so small? . . .'

'The entrance to hell has this peculiarity, it is extremely elastic,' I explained. 'Without any trouble, and with very little pain, it can admit the most voluminous demon provided that he does not set about his work roughly . . . It is only the first time that it hurts a little, and the intense pleasure soon makes up for the slight pain! . . . And now you know how, in order to be perfectly happy, a man and a girl behave together. You are, I expect, already much more learned in these matters than the most learned of your companions but this is only the beginning! For besides putting the devil into hell there are many other caresses by which the supreme pleasure, which Father Rustique and Alibech enjoyed so often, may be obtained by the excitement of the senses, and in these ways I hope to instruct you too, my darlings; you are not tired?'

From their sweet little mouths issued a double 'oh!' of protest which made it quite unnecessary for me to pursue that point further, and besides, at that moment, the door opened, after the usual knocks, and Madame rejoined us.

4

DANCES

'Now,' said she, 'if you will allow me, I will introduce to you my assistants.'

And turning to Evelyn and Nora she continued:

'You will have before you, young ladies, the pick of the beauty and grace of Paris. I make a point of gathering round me only girls who are really beautiful, well educated, and of charming disposition and character. They are well trained and full of tact, and I can assure you that you will in no way suffer by making their acquaintance, but quite the contrary.'

My two little friends bowed somewhat nervously: I pressed them to me affectionately and whispered:

'Even if they are all this, you surpass them a hundred-fold!'

A fond look from each of them seemed to thank me and Madame conducted us to the Drawing-Room.

Here there was none of that bad taste which is so often to be seen in houses of this description.

The temple of the rue Ch– is the abode of good style. There are not too many mirrors and too much tawdry gilding about. All the furniture and fittings are of the best class and seem designed to set off to the best advantage the pretty faces and the sparkling eyes which are to be encountered there.

The Drawing-Room was already occupied, for we found there about a dozen of the young women of the establishment – or rather I might say of the young girls, for the eldest of them was not more than twenty-five, and some of the younger ones seemed as indeed I knew them to be, considerably under twenty-one, which is the youngest at which legally a girl may enter a 'bordel' in Paris – who rose to meet us as we entered. They were all charmingly dressed and showed not the slightest signs of being what they really were. One would have taken them for society girls who had met together at a friend's house for a little gossip and music. And indeed one of them was seated at a fine Erard grand which, draped with rich material and half surrounded with little palm trees, occupied one corner of the room. She was just finishing the last bars of the adagio of a sonata as we entered and it was evident by her touch and execution that she was a first-rate pianist.

Among the first of those who came to meet us was my little friend Rose, of whom I have spoken; next to her was her special friend Marie, with whom Rose always liked to 'work' in case, as so often happened, a visitor wished to be 'entertained' by two girls at once.

Madame R introduced the girls to us singly and announced us as her good friend 'whom they all knew' and his two nieces.

'And now, girls,' said Madame, 'perhaps you will entertain us with a little music and dancing. I am sure these young ladies will be surprised and delighted with the way in which you dance the Italian dances for example! Blanche, will you play us something?'

'Certainly, Madame,' replied the girl who had been at the piano. 'An Italian valse? Something dreamy? . . .'

'Yes, that's it!' I approved smiling; 'something decidedly "dreamy"!'

'Very well!' said Blanche with a merry laugh; 'I will play you "Surgente di amore" . . . "The Springs of Love." '

'No,' said Madame, 'let us proceed by degrees. Begin with "Tesoro mio"; then you will give us "Io t'amo" and finally will come "Surgente di amore".'

The programme being thus arranged, Blanche took her place at the piano, five couples of dancers were formed, and the impassioned strains of the celebrated valses 'Tesoro mio' and 'Io t'amo' regulated the beautiful dance, quite 'proper' at present but highly voluptuous.

In 'Io t'amo', especially towards the end, the sensuous nature of the Piedmontese valse became more noticeable. Rose and Marie especially were dancing with delightful skill; it really seemed that they understood the most refined shades of voluptuousness. Instead of continuing to turn round and round in the valse as their companions did, they seemed to sway from side to side with a delightful undulating motion of their bodies and of their splendid bottoms, while, face to face, or side by side, with their heads thrown back, and their nostrils palpitating, their open lips seemed to invite hot burning kisses.

I was seated on a sofa with, of course, Evelyn and Nora on each side of me, and Madame was sitting near us.

I could feel my two little companions vibrate in unison with Rose and Marie, whom I had pointed out to them as the couple most deserving of their attention.

How could I longer restrain the intense ardour which was devouring me!

The charming freshness of Evelyn and Nora, and their sweet confidence in me simply drove me mad. I could feel that their virgin modesty was intensely excited and I thought with delight of their sweet young bodies, never yet strained by look or touch, which were experiencing such strange sensations, – sensations which I knew were to be so much more acute in a few minute's time.

'It's pretty, isn't it?' I asked softly.

'Oh! yes,' said Evelyn trembling.

Her lips were slightly parted over her beautiful teeth and her nostrils quivered as though inhaling some rich perfume. Nora whispered, almost touching my cheek:

'Uncle Jack! It's only today for the first time that I realise what dancing really is!'

'You darling! You would like to dance too, wouldn't you?'

'Oh, no! I . . . I should be afraid!'

'No, you wouldn't be afraid, nor would you, Evelyn, would you?'

'Oh, no, not a bit,' said Evelyn eagerly, 'but I should like to dance with Rose, if I may.'

'Certainly you shall dance with her, and you, Nora, with Marie, and all the others, except the pianist, shall leave the room if you like.'

'Oh, yes! oh, yes, that's just what we should like!'

The dance was drawing to a close, and a most voluptuous one, although Rose and Marie had not given one another the supreme embrace, following in this the directions of Madame.

I whispered a few words in the good lady's ear; she got up and spoke for a moment to the girls who retired with the exception of Rose, Marie and Blanche.

When we were alone I said to Rose:

'I shall be very much obliged if you will have a turn with Evelyn, Rose, and you, Marie, will take charge of Nora. They are charmed with you and are delighted with your way of dancing!'

'Oh,' said Rose, 'that's nothing; we will show the young ladies something much nicer than that! Now Blanche, play us the "Surgente di amore"!'

And Blanche began to play it.

At first things did not go too well, especially with Nora, who was less quick than Evelyn in accommodating herself to the new measure. But soon I had the intense pleasure of seeing my two nieces dancing as gracefully and, I might almost say, as lasciviously as their delighted instructress.

And soon the style changed.

Up to this point Rose and Marie had held their partners in the usual way, but now, placing their arms more firmly round their waists, they pressed their trembling bodies more closely to their own. . . .

And then indeed the dance became almost maddening in its refined lasciviousness. Of course Rose and Marie were past mistresses in the art and seemed to take a real pleasure in initiating the two charming flappers. Pressed close together, a thigh was now advanced and inserted between those of Evelyn and Nora, their bodies and breasts seemed to form one and the warm breath of the partners was mingled. Slowly in this position they revolved for a few moments, when it became evident that the voluptuous valse had justified its title and that – for the first time as I supposed in the case of my little friends – the springs of love were opened.

The happy climax was reached just as the last strains of the dance were dying away. Rose and Marie at the critical moment had led their partners in front of Madame and myself as we sat on the sofa. I saw suddenly, and at the same moment, Evelyn and Nora fall forward and collapse in the arms of the two girls: their knees seemed to bend forward, their loins were arched in, their thighs gripped as though in a vice the thigh of their partner, and the convulsive jerks of their bottoms, plainly visible under their thin dresses, left no doubt that the sluices were opened and that the tide of love was flowing freely. They would have certainly fallen if Rose and Marie had not supported them and half carried them to a seat, where they remained for a few moments as though dead.

They however soon recovered and seemed a little ashamed of their weakness. I went and took them by the hand and led them to the sofa where I had been sitting.

'What has happened?' I asked smiling.

They were equally unable to find an answer, so I came to their assistance.

'Don't try to put me off with some fairy tale,' I said gaily: 'I will explain to you what has happened.'

Rose and Marie were talking together at the end of the room and Madame had gone up to the pianist to congratulate her on the success of her playing.

'Dancing undertaken in a certain manner,' I said, 'is naturally conducive to pleasure in the sense that it excites those parts of the body which are the seat of the novel sensations which you have just experienced. You know the parts that I mean?'

Silence.

'You know,' I continued, 'that these are the central parts of the body: the loins, the lower part of the belly, the thighs, the bottom, all nervous sensations are centred here. But when the dance is conducted as it was just now, when the bodies touch – still more when it is a man and a girl who are dancing together – when the belly of one is pressed against the belly of the other and when the thigh of one is inserted and rubs against the thighs of the other and the lower parts of the belly, thus exciting the treasures which are hidden there . . .'

'Uncle Jack!' sighed Nora, 'you are driving me mad!'

'Don't interrupt, Nora,' said Evelyn with a quick and tender glance, 'go on, Uncle Jack, all this is most interesting!'

'Then there takes place what has just occurred to both of you: a prolonged and infinitely delicious spasm, and which – with certain variations – is always produced when one "spends" as it is called, this is to say when one enjoys the sensation which you have just experienced. Evelyn dear, tell me openly exactly what you felt.'

'For my part,' said Evelyn softly, 'what had the great effect on me was the rubbing . . . Oh! how shall I explain it?'

'Of the thigh?'

'No . . . of the belly. It seemed to me that my very being was attracted by Rosie's belly: I seemed to feel it naked under my dress! . . .'

'There's nothing peculiar about that, darling. I have often felt that remarkable attraction myself.'

'But how can you feel, you a man, what we

girls have just felt, as you are not made as we are?'

'Pleasure is all one. Men and women feel it equally and just in the same way. You have, however, one great advantage over us! Your pleasure, otherwise called your "spending", is much more prolonged than ours and does not take it out of you nearly so much.'

'Really?'

I could see that this piece of information interested the two dears immensely. Evelyn continued:

'You will think me inquisitive, Uncle Jack, but I should like to know how it was that you experienced what you were saying about . . . the belly.'

'I have often experienced it,' I said. 'My governess was a *strict disciplinarian* and she used to often whip me. Now, she had a way of turning the punishment of a whipping into a delightful pleasure for me. When she whipped me she used to take down my trousers and turn up my shirt and then place me across her knees from which she had removed her skirt and petticoat. Thus my bare belly seemed to be pressed against hers and caused me such pleasure as to quite outweigh the smarting of the birch; and I enjoyed this all the more because a whipping in itself has peculiarly erotic effects.'

'Erotic?' said Nora.

'Yes, darling, erotic means having relation to sensual love.'

'Really? And so a whipping raises a sensation

of love! Oh, how funny! I should never have believed such a thing if you hadn't told us!'

'But it's true all the same, you dears, and you will be able to test it for yourselves before long . . . and I can assure you that you will surprised at the results.'

Meanwhile Evelyn was making a curious little grimace which I noticed.

'What is it, Evelyn?' I asked softly.

She blushed deeply and murmured:

'I should . . . I should like . . .'

'And so should I,' said Nora naively.

I was amused at their enbarrassment and insisted.

'You would like what? Come, out with it!'

'I should like to go for a moment to . . . to a bedroom.'

'Oh!' said I, 'I know what's the matter!'

'Uncle Jack! please.'

'There's nothing to blush about in that. I'll bet that, as they say in French, you've done "pipi" . . .'

The two little darlings hid their blushes in their hands.

'Of course that's it,' I continued. 'Well, my dears, don't be alarmed. You require certain ablutions, no doubt, but you have not "done pipi". What has happened to you is what always happens when one enjoys the supreme pleasure, there has been what is called an emission of love-juice. In the man, this juice shot out by the devil into the hell of a woman is the liquid of Life, the liquid in which reside the elements of a baby.

Now, go with Rose and Marie and they will conduct you to a place where you will find everything you require.'

At a sign from Madame, to whom I had hinted the requirements of my little friends, Rose and Marie came up to them and led them from the room.

Blanche had already retired and I was left alone with the good lady of the house. I took advantage of this to thank her for the complete success of the first part of the programme.

'The second part will be much more pleasant for you,' she assured me. 'Everything is ready and Rose has received all necessary instructions.'

5

THE SPANKING ROOM

When my two charming 'nieces' and Rose returned, Madame conducted us to the Spanking Room. It was a large room hung with dark yellow velvet. Ladders of varnished wood, the bars of which were here and there provided with straps, a wooden horse covered with soft leather, a cupboard containing every kind of instrument of flagellation, a long wide sofa, a narrow oak bench, both of them furnished with straps, and finally the whipping chair formed the furniture of this comfortable apartment from which no cries or appeals could escape.

Not that it is a room of torture, far from that, but, as I explained to the girls later, there are certain refined voluptuaries who never feel the supreme pleasure so keenly as when they have been severely scourged by a female hand.

We must of course admit that there are tastes of all kinds.

As soon as we entered the room Madame left

us to the tender care of Rose who alone had accompanied us.

My little friend invited us to be seated and then said:

'I must tell you, young ladies and Monsieur, that it is a rule of the house that no visitor may enter the Spanking Room without receiving a whipping. It is a tribute which must be paid! With which of you shall I begin?'

Evelyn and Nora, crimson with confusion, declared that 'they would be much too much ashamed to be whipped before me.'

At this Rose laughed heartily.

'Really?' she said. 'Perhaps you are afraid that your uncle would be shocked at the sight of your charms? . . . If that is so, you can banish all fear. Monsieur is no novice I can assure you. He has seen many a whipped bottom. And I don't mind admitting that he has seen mine dancing under the rod not so very long ago.'

'But,' objected Evelyn, 'it must hurt terribly!' Rose's laughter increased.

'Not at all, not at all!' she said. 'Please remember that we are here *for our pleasure and not for our pain*! Don't be alarmed, young ladies, and make up your minds to go through it. One thing is certain, and that is that you will not leave this room without having had a whipping, nor will your uncle either!'

'Oh, for my part,' I said, 'I will gladly submit to the rules of the house.'

'Then,' said Evelyn, 'you have it first!'

'No,' said Rose, 'that would be breaking the

rules. We must always begin with a visitor who is making a first visit to the establishment.'

'Evelyn,' said I, 'I will give you my word of honour that I will go through it after you and Nora. And besides didn't you tell me that "you were prepared for anything"? If you want to understand things you must learn by personal experience . . . And I assure you that you won't suffer any pain, but quite the contrary!'

'But you will see me!'

'And have I not some little claim to such a delicious reward?'

'And Nora will have it after me?'

'Yes, after you, and I after Nora!'

'Oh, good heavens, very well then; do with me as you like! . . .'

Assisted by Rose I led her to the arm chair. The seat consists, so to speak, of two arms placed close together, hollowed out like a gutter, and thickly padded. We directed Evelyn to kneel down on it and this she did without much hesitation.

Promptly Rose fastened her legs to the arms by means of two broad webbing straps, and then directed her to place her arms round the back of the chair: these she fastened securely at the wrists by means of another strap.

Evelyn then noticed that her stomach was resting on a sort of velvet cushion fixed at the bottom of the back of the chair.

'What is it placed there for?' she asked, a little frightened without knowing exactly why.

'To support you, darling,' I said. 'Now don't be afraid!'

Touching a lever Rose set the back of the chair in motion.

It fell slowly, but steadily, backwards, drawing with it the upper part of the astonished Evelyn's body.

A cry of distress issued from her pretty lips, and Nora frightened too, rose from her seat and seemed inclined to cry out.

'Don't be frightened,' I said quickly. 'Be a good girl, Nora. I've told you that no harm shall happen to Evelyn: you can have complete confidence in me.'

Evelyn meanwhile, continued to utter little cries of terror which became more plaintive when the back of the chair continuing to fall backwards, the dear girl found herself falling forwards quite gently it is true, and without her fastened limbs or her body suffering any pain whatsoever. The downward movement only ceased when the back was almost parallel with the floor, and as the arms had risen as the back fell, Evelyn found herself exactly in the position as if she had been on all fours, that is to say her bottom was raised in a way most admirably adapted for a whipping. This position in itself was already extremely exciting for Nora and me, the spectators – especially for me – but what was it compared with what I was about to see! . . . The mere idea of this made me tremble with desire. Evelyn, on finding herself thus exposed, felt a very natural agony of shame. She cried out more loudly and her lovely face expressed a regular terror when she found herself thus placed with her head lower than her heels.

Rose gently reassured her.

'Oh! Miss Evelyn,' she said, 'you are not going to cry out like a little baby, surely! . . . You know that it's only fun! If you really deserved to be punished and if we wished to do so, we should not take so much care to make you comfortable, should we? You will see how curious it is and what strange and powerful emotions this new experience provokes . . . Now, be a good girl, and we will begin the operation.'

'Ah, yes! Monsieur Quatrefois will see your pretty little bottom! He will see it birched! And what if he does! I don't suppose that you imagine that it is the first time that he has seen such a thing! I can assure you that your bottom will not be the first that he has seen under such conditions; will it, Monsieur?'

'I'm obliged to confess that it will not!' said I laughing.

But the shame which is inseparable from the 'preparation' for a whipping had now taken complete possession of Evelyn. Her face was crimson and sweet little tears appeared on her long eyelashes and this attitude of humiliation, I must confess, gave me infinitely more pleasure than if she had taken the situation as a matter of course, to be merely laughed at.

Rose delicately seized between the thumb and finger of each hand the edge of her light skirt and turned it up slowly over the patient's shoulders. Evelyn uttered such a cry of distress that, if I had

173

not restrained myself, I should have flung myself on my knees before her and kissed her little lips, so pretty in their timid fear, in order to comfort her.

'Oh, what are you going to do?' she sighed.

'I am about to uncover this part of you, Miss,' said Rose smiling. 'You don't suppose that we are going to whip you over your petticoats, do you?'

'Evelyn, darling,' I said in my turn, 'if you really wish to know everything, you must submit to everything. And it's all the more easy to do this because, I assure you, it isn't a punishment that Rose is about to inflict on you but a most delightful caress!'

'Oh, I believe you . . . But it seems so dreadful! So shocking! Oh, do get it over quickly! . . .'

Rose, highly amused, proceeded to raise the soft petticoat and then her light and skilful hands sought out, under the waist and the upturned clothes, the buttons of the drawers.

And, as is always the case, this search was the beginning of the excitement, and what a novel excitement it was, for Evelyn, I could see it by the nervous trembling which shook her charming posteriors, still protected by their thin covering. I could not take my eyes from these splendid rotundities, the bold roundness and fullness of which were thus suddenly revealed to me. The drawers, made of the finest lawn, were open – as the drawers of every self-respecting flapper should be – and at the bottom of the slit, near the thighs, a little end of the chemise peeped out, and trembled like a little tail. How I should have loved to raise this little tail and insert beneath it an investigating finger or an inquisitive glance! The drawers, very full in the legs – although at this moment tightly stretched by the jutting out position of their sumptuous contents – were slit up the side to a certain point and this opening was fastened at the top by a large bow of rose coloured satin. Rich Valenciennes lace, forming an edging fell down over the well formed calves encased in their charming open-work black silk-stockings. They were as pretty a pair of drawers as you could want to see, and I could not help wondering if Evelyn, anticipating what was in store for her, had put them on for my benefit, and if I should find that Nora was equally dainty in her undies when her turn came to display them. Meanwhile Rose, having found the buttons, slipped the drawers down to the knees, and then slowly, and with gestures which seemed almost religious, raised the fine crêpe chemise and turned it up over the shoulders with the petticoats.

It was indeed a lovely sight which presented itself.

To be sure, I have seen the bottom of many girls and women in my time, and as, no doubt, many of my readers have been equally fortunate, I see no reason to deny it. But this time I felt more deeply moved than ever before, and with good reason, for Evelyn's bottom was an absolute marvel – and it is so still, I may say at once!

What painter, were he at the very top of his profession, could produce that delightful fruit of pink and white flesh, so attractive and so delicate in its development? . . . But even if he did succeed in this task he would only have produced an incomplete work, infinitely inferior to the reality: there would be wanting the life, manifesting itself in those quiverings and tremblings the mere sight of which intoxicate one. There would be wanting above all that imponderable thing, the feeling of seeing, of admiring, a virgin's bottom, a bottom pure and fresh, absolutely chaste and never yet uncovered – at least to the eyes of a man – never yet soiled by the slightest touch, I gazed upon it with an almost religious emotion, with which was mingled, let it be said, no slight admixture of hot desire.

I did not dare to ask Rose to allow me to whip the delightful treasure, but at the moment I made up my mind to use my utmost endeavour to be able to do so at some time or other: whether my hopes were ever to be realised – this, as Rudyard Kipling would say, 'is another story'. Rose, who no doubt was not quite affected in the same way as myself, had taken from the cupboard two instruments of flagellation. She placed one on the seat near the armchair and held the other in her hand.

The first was the classic instrument, a birch rod, formed of thin elastic twigs about two feet long, bound together for half their length and covered with broad red ribbon.

The other, which she held in her hand, was a

martinet or cat-o-nine-tails, but of a kind that would have been of no terror to a naughty boy. While the wooden handle was bound round with soft leather, the six leather thongs, about a foot long, were covered with crimson velvet.

In this way the severity of the whipping – a severity which is always possible as the result of the excitement of the operator – would be so much diminished that the only effects of a love whipping would be an extreme irritation of the senses and an intense desire for an affective relief.

I thought that Rose was now ready to put an end to Evelyn's agony of mind by proceeding to whip her at once, but such was not the case . . . Turning a little handle at the side of the chair she caused the arms – to which Evelyn's knees were strapped – to open with the result that the lovely girl's thighs were forced wide apart. Nor was this the only result.

At first surprised, and then really frightened, Evelyn uttered such cries of terror that Rose was quite dismayed.

'Oh, do be quiet,' she said impatiently, 'you really are too tiresome! Let me tell you, miss, that if it was left to me I should give you something to cry out about!'

'Come, Evelyn, come!' I said in my turn. 'You know it's not serious. Don't make such a fuss you are not going to get hurt! . . .'

Nora was sitting by my side, and we were just behind Evelyn. Rose was standing by her left side in such a way that Nora and I could admire in their most intimate details the treasures of our little companion.

What first attracted my attention was the tight little pinky-brown button hole which Evelyn tried in vain to conceal by closing the cheeks of her bottom . . . The attempt met with no success owing to the wide stretch of the thighs. Underneath appeared brown curls, as fine and soft as silk, which grew thicker as they ascended till they formed a thick downy fleece. In this nestled, like two rolled up petals of a fresh crimson rose seeking to hide itself in the shade, the tightly closed lips of the virgin springs of love.

How compact and fresh it all seemed! And how profoundly moved I was at the sight of such lovely charms so beautifully – and so indecently – displayed. My nerves were on the tingle and my blood seemed to course in hot waves through my veins . . . By me sat Nora, her face scarlet! She had taken my hand, the little darling, and was pressing it convulsively.

'Nora!' I muttered, 'my darling! I am just in the condition that Father Rustique was; do you understand me? The devil is aroused!'

She moved uneasily on her chair, blushed still more deeply and stammered:

'The devil? . . . Oh, Uncle Jack! . . .'

She lowered her eyes in confusion. I gently guided her hand to the spot where the devil was making his presence felt. At first she seemed to wish to withdraw it, but I held the soft warm hand there by gently firmness.

'Do you feel it, dear? Tell me if you feel it?'

'Yes . . . Oh, yes, I feel it,' she sighed.

I felt her tremble delightfully but I did not wish to push the experience any further for the moment. And besides, Rose was now beginning to whip Evelyn, whose bottom at once began to dance while she uttered little cries, whether of fear or pleasure it would not have been easy to decide. Skilfully handled the velvet covered thongs of the martinet wrapped themselves round the plump and muscular cheeks of Evelyn's bottom.

Pretty red stripes soon began to appear and presently, the by no means severe and most delicately applied whipping began to produce the desired effect, that is to say an intensely sensual sensation.

Evelyn ceased to utter her little cries. Only 'Ah! ah! ah! . . .' escaped from her lips as each stroke fell, while her eyes assumed a dreamy look. Finally the intense itching sensation became so unbearable over the whole of her tender bottom that she experienced an uncomfortable desire to be whipped more severely.

She herself assured me of these impressions later on, as did Nora, but I need hardly say that I was well acquainted with them myself. Evelyn, by then, having ceased to cry out, now found herself a prey to the very demon of lasciviousness. Her bottom was quivering and dancing in the most indecent manner and she had quite given up all attempts to hide from us the most tender and secret parts of her lovely body. Her breathing became quick and sharp, her burning sensations seemed to increase her beauty and impassioned words escaped from her red and parted lips.

'Ah! Go on! Go on! Harder! Oh! It's maddening! Oh! It's delicious! Oh! Go on! Harder still! Ah! Ah! . . .'

Rose, alert and intensely interested, increased the severity of her strokes, knowing well that the only effect would be to excite, and not to damage, the tender flesh. Suddenly dropped the martinet and took up the birch, judging no doubt that the glowing bottom was now prepared for the more severe attack of the supple twigs.

And she was right. The elastic birch, curling round the beautiful trembling and quivering globes, came down with a hiss on the hot crimson flesh. Here and there dark red stripes appeared, but Evelyn, beside herself with the intensity of the sensations which she was now experiencing for the first time, uttered not the slightest complaint.

Virgin though she was, under the effects of the whipping, she had lost all modesty and I am certain that at this moment she would have gladly yielded to me her maidenhead.

But I had promised Madame R that the girls should leave her house virgins in body and I was determined to keep my promise.

When Rose saw that her patient had reached the paroxysm of passion she dropped the birch, took up the martinet and, with gentle and carefully directed strokes, began to whip her between the legs. . . .

The velvet covered thongs, following the deep

valley, struck, or rather caressed, the soft treasures which I have described.

The effect was really astonishing.

Evelyn stiffened the whole of her body in a supreme spasm. With nervous contractions she agitated her thighs and bottom, while a deep sob of pleasure issued from her lips and was repeated again and again.

Nora, surprised and a little frightened, pressed close up to me. I felt her supple young body against my shoulder, a sensation which was not calculated to diminish the fire which was consuming me. I passed my arm round her waist and gently fondled the magnificent rotundities which I was looking forward to be able to admire in a few moments as conveniently as those of her friend.

'Are you wondering what Evelyn's sensations are?' I asked in a low voice.

'Yes . . .' she asmitted.

'Well, she has been having a perfectly blissful time. Would you have thought that a whipping was able to produce such a wonderful effect?'

'No, indeed, Uncle Jack!'

'You little darling! You shall try it yourself in a moment. It is not only by putting the devil into hell that one can feel this delightful sensation as I have told you, and now you have the proof of it! Oh, no, there are many other ways, I can assure you.'

Evelyn remained for some little time overcome by the swoon into which the supreme excitement of the voluptuous whipping had plunged her. She continued to sigh, softly and Nora, reassured by what I had just said with regard to Evelyn's sensations, suddenly began to laugh heartily. This rather surprised me, having regard to her recent emotion and I asked her.

'What's the matter Nora? What makes you laugh so?'

'It's Evelyn,' she said, bursting out again. 'The spectacle is so comic! Oh, how funny she is. Look how she is wriggling her . . . her bottom, and how she is showing . . . everything and so comically too!'

'Oh, Miss Nora,' said Rose assuming the magisterial tone of an irate school-mistress, 'you are wrong to laugh at Miss Evelyn. In a few moments you will find yourself precisely in the position that she is now in, and a little later you will behave exactly as you have seen her behave! All those who enter this room go through the same contortions and utter the same sighs! I will now unfasten Miss Evelyn and prepare you; now come along!'

Nora, confused and crimson with emotion, wriggled on her seat and pressed more closely up to me.

'Oh, no!' she murmured: 'I won't!'

She made an adorable little grimace, so charming that I felt tempted to softly bite her lovely little mouth to punish her for being so insubordinate.

'You won't?' I said in feigned astonishment, 'Oh! what a horrid word! Let me tell you that no well-behaved young lady in a spanking room ever says "I will" or "I won't": merely for this you will have to mount the chair, so come along!'

I took her gently in my arms to move her towards the chair but she resisted a little, and this gave me the chance of feeling her supple plump body under the thin material of her dress.

'It will have to be,' I said. 'Be a good girl, Nora, and don't compel me to use force. You know that a girl ought to obey her uncle, don't you?'

'Now, Miss Nora, come at once,' said Rose in her turn. 'Now, it will be Miss Evelyn who will laugh at you!'

'Indeed, Nora, you surprise me,' said Evelyn, 'what has become of all your old pluck?'

'Miss Nora used to be brave, then?' said Rose jeeringly. 'What a change!'

'Yes, indeed, she was,' continued Evelyn, 'we used to consider her the bravest girl in the school.'

'I am just the same!' said she, turning up her sweet little nose and looking at us each in turn with her great blue eyes, more blue by reason of the crimson in her cheeks. 'And that there may be no doubt about it I will show it to you too!'

I burst out laughing at these words. The little darling! She did not see the humour of her remark in her innocence.

For, indeed, if she was to show us *how brave she was*, she would have to show *it* to us, namely that which I was longing to see. Of her own accord she knelt on the arms of the chair which had been restored to their position by Rose who immediately strapped her knees and hands as she had done in the case of Evelyn.

It was quickly done, for Rose, like myself, found an added excitement from the semblance of resistance which the capricious Nora offered.

Immediately the back of the chair was tilted backwards, the arms were raised and the machinery which operated them was set in motion, in spite of the agonised appeals of Nora.

'Oh, yes! you may cry! You see what you have let yourself in for!' said Rose. 'You will have to show *everything* at once as a punishment for your resistance. And I am sure that we are about to see something that will be well worth our careful attention, for you are charmingly pretty, Miss Nora!'

The little rogue had murmured this in the culprit's ear and I saw that she had taken advantage of this to gently bite the lobe of this ear, which is one of the most exciting caresses that I know, especially when, at the same time, the hand of the operator 'is at work' either under the petticoats or inside the trousers.

Now, Rose's hand 'was at work' under Nora's petticoats in a way which, as she admitted to me later, at once aroused an extraordinary sensation of pleasure.

The skilful ministrant to my desires unbuttoned the drawers and let them down and then, slipping her hand under the chemise , she softly stroked and tickled the trembling globes of Nora's posterior charms.

The strange and novel sensation seemed to

drive the sweet girl almost mad. Little cries and entreaties mingled with signs were evidence of this, as well as the undulations of the loins and the trembling of the bottom which always result in the case of one not accustomed to be thus handled.

But Rose knew that she was not there to gratify her own pleasure.

Evidently delighted at having thus excited Nora, she stood up, came behind her and turned up the petticoats.

If Nora's bottom was apparently less muscular than Evelyn's it seemed to be just as attractive in the harmony of its curves and the full development of its sumptuous globes.

I have said that the girls of Madame X's school were well known throughout Paris for the smartness of their dressing and Nora's undies were as dainty as those of her young companion. The drawers, of lawn like those of Evelyn, were not hanging loosely round her knees, and for the first time I caught a glimpse of the soft white flesh between the tops of her stockings and the edges of her chemise.

A moment later and Rose had turned up the chemise and immediately were displayed before me, delightful in the indecent completeness of their exposure, the beauties which so far I had only pictured in my mind. Here, indeed, was the eternal fruit offered to the appetite of man, that wonderful fruit which, from the distant time of the earthly Paradise, has offered itself to the pious hands of the lovers of Eve.

But had there been but one fruit in that famous garden like to that which Nora now offered to our enraptured gaze, its mere presence would have explained the madness of Adam.

It was a combination of form and colour calculated to amaze and delight the most experienced painter of the nude. The skin was so soft and fine that one felt a desire to kneel down before the beautiful globes and bite boldly into them and perhaps to smother them with kisses, or to make them quiver with the gentle tickling of the fingers or under the stinging embraces of an elastic birch. In the shady valley, where grew a fair and downy moss, thanks to the wide separation of the thighs, I could admire the rosy virgin jewels which seemed to invite my lips.

'Nora,' I said, 'I can assure you that you and Evelyn are perfectly adorable from all points of view. How on earth, darling, could you wish to hide such treasures from us? It would have been a crime Rose wouldn't it?'

'A regular crime!' said Rose.

There was no doubt that she was very much excited by the fair charms – 'Sithone acandidiora nive' as Ovid would have said – of Nora, and I could not help suspecting in her certain Sapphic tastes which I had never been aware of before.

Rose now took up the martinet and, while with her left hand she softly caressed Nora's cheek – very sensitive as I could see to the gentle tickling – she began to whip her bottom, following the same method as she had employed in the 'correction' of Evelyn. From the very first, Nora showed by her contortions and lascivious movements that, though a blonde, she was as sensitive to a whipping as the dark and more highly strung Evelyn. For a long time it seemed Rose continued to whip her, then she subsituted the birch for the martinet when she judged that the right moment had come.

Presently the velvet covered thongs of the martinet resumed their delightful task, working up to the final scene. The tight little button-hole and the rosy cheeks, as fresh and pouting and closed as Evelyn's eyes, received the last tender strokes which brought on the inevitable crisis.

Nora's whole body quivered and contracted and then . . . jerk . . . jerk . . ., a panting 'O . . . h! O . . . h, a . . . h' and a deep sob of delight marked the crowning point of her enjoyment.

Standing just behind her, with her bottom and thighs arranged in such a position that we could see every detail of the young woman's emotion, we watched the love-fit run its course for a full minute, then the sweet girl seemed to collapse, overcome by pleasure and confusion.

Delightful power of youth! How much, as I watched this charming scene, I regretted my young years when the same simple cause would have produced on my nature the same pleasant effects. But alas, it now required more than a mere whipping to produce in me the final spasm.

Nora, half laughing and half weeping, so intense had been her enjoyment, was unfastened and prettily proceeded to adjust the disorder of her raiment.

'And now, Monsieur Quatrefois,' said Rose shaking a finger at me, 'it's your turn! Oh, yes! and you deserve it. I'm certain that what you have been watching with so much interest has made you feel very naughty! Let me see!'

Boldly she came up to me and unbuttoned the front of my trousers with her soft and skilful little hand. Then I felt it creep in under my shirt, just tickle for a moment my balls, and then proceed to test the condition of my tool.

'Ah, I thought as much!' said she. 'Now, sir you will have to be whipped: come and kneel down here at once without making any fuss about it.'

It would have been ungracious on my part to refuse after what Evelyn and Nora had been through, so I at once did as Rose directed. Immediately she fastened me down securely and I felt her active fingers unbutton my braces and let down my trousers. Next moment I was aware that I was uncovered from my loins to my knees, and close to me, highly excited and blushing divinely, were Evelyn and Nora, examining me attentively with a somewhat nervous smile.

'Is it I who am to whip you?' asked Rose with a meaning air.

Immediately objections were raised to this.

'Oh! No! Mademoiselle. Do let us do it! You will show us how, won't you?'

Of course this was just what I wanted and I asked Rose to accede to their wishes. Rose, highly amused, handed the martinet to Evelyn who, on this occassion, did not fail to assert her right of priority! Evelyn looked first at the martinet and then at my behind and it was evident that she was shy about beginning the operation.

'Well, Miss Evelyn? . . .' asked Rose smiling, 'what are you waiting for?'

'I . . . oh . . . Do you think, Mademoiselle, that it will hurt Uncle Jack?'

'Just as it hurt you; no more and no less!'

'But . . . but where shall I strike?'

'Well! It seems to me that the right place is conveniently displayed! Right across the bottom, to be sure! And another on the lower part, just where you see his bottom join his thighs; that's where it is most sensitive. If you want to produce the greatest feeling of shame and also the highest pitch of sensual excitement it is just across the lower part of the bottom and the upper part of the thighs that you should apply the strokes. But now begin and I will direct you as you proceed.'

And Evelyn began to whip me.

Thanks to the velvet covering of the thongs the whipping was a mere caress and I had all the impression of being whipped without any of the pain, while I had the special delight of knowing that it was Evelyn – and later on Nora – who was inflicting the pleasant punishment.

When the two little dears had well warmed my bottom, Rose took from them the martinet and handed the birch to Evelyn.

'Now' said she, 'follow my instruction carefully, give me your left hand. Do you feel something?'

'Oh, good heavens!' exclaimed Evelyn, drawing back her hand quickly. 'Oh, how it frightened me: Whatever is it? . . .'

'Look and see!'

Rose made Evelyn and Nora stoop down and showed them, standing up along my belly, long and stiff and in a fine state of erection, my devil just in the condition of that of Father Rustique at the moment when he plunged it into Alibech's hell.

'Oh!' said Nora, 'it's a real one! A real live one!'

'A real live devil!' repeated Evelyn much moved. 'It's the first we have ever seen, isn't it Nora?'

'Yes,' said Nora. 'But I wish I could get a better view of it . . . It doesn't look dangerous! The very first!'

'I'm delighted that it should be mine which has that honour,' I murmured, 'you can touch it, it's not dangerous, I can assure you!'

'No, indeed,' said Rose: 'it can't bite or scratch, but I rather think that, before long the young ladies will find that it can spit pretty freely!'

This sally of wit on the part of Rose made us both laugh rather at the surprise of the two girls who were unable as yet to appreciate the joke. Both of them wanted to caress it at the same time, just as one caresses a pretty and curious animal.

The condition into which all this put me can be easily imagined!

'That's all very well, young ladies,' said Rose. 'But we must not forget that your uncle has not yet had the end of his whipping. Now, Miss Evelyn, place yourself here, on his left. That's right. Now pass your hand under him, and take firm hold of his devil as you call it. Yes, that's it . . . Now that you've got hold of him, birch his bottom again for him nicely, laying the strokes on harder as you go.'

Evelyn obeyed. The sensation of having my prick thus held in her little hand drove me mad, and as the strokes of the birch fell I began to work my bottom backwards and forwards.

The inevitable result would soon have followed if Rose, who had a new idea, had not withdrawn Evelyn's hand.

'Whip him well under the cheeks of his bottom . . . Steady . . . gently . . . not too hard: wait, I will open the arms of the chair wider for you . . . There, now whip him well down the crack . . .'

I began to pant and writhe with pleasure but had not quite reached the spending point. Then I heard Rose speak again.

'Now, it's your turn to birch him, Miss Nora. Do as Miss Evelyn did. But there are no fixed rules. The operator should perform as she thinks best: she should try to put as much variety and personal charm as possible into the performance.'

'Yes, yes,' I said. 'I will explain all that to them later. Now, Nora darling, whip me well.'

My bottom seemed fairly on fire so delightfully was my skin burning and Nora, encouraged by what Rose had just said, tried a method of her own.

She passed her left hand well down under my belly and with the tips of her fingers began to tickle my balls and up and down the shaft of my prick, while at the same time she applied the birch to my bottom in such a way that Rose soon saw that I should not be able to restrain myself much longer if my sweet little tormentor continued her operations. She therefore removed her hand as she had done with Evelyn.

'That will do for the present,' said she, 'otherwise I shall not be able to show you something in a moment which will interest you very much.'

'Oh, what is it?' asked the two girls together.

'You shall see. But first let us unfasten your uncle.'

'Oh! But! . . .' exclaimed Evelyn, 'it's not finished. He . . . he hasn't . . . felt what we felt just now; both of us!'

'Ah!' said Rose laughing, 'that's just what I want to show you! . . . There! . . . Your bottom is beautifully red, Monsieur Quatrefois. You have had a real good whipping but, then, you deserved it. Confess it and come and receive your pardon with a kiss from your three tormentors!'

I made haste to obey, and I enjoyed from the crimson and fresh lips of my two little flappers, as well as from those of my more experienced young friend, three of the most delightful kisses that I have ever had in my life!

6

A LESSON IN MALE ANATOMY

Without giving me time to button up my trousers, Rose, followed by Evelyn and Nora who were most curious to see what was going to happen, pushed me towards a door which opened into a sort of small alcove. It formed so to speak a kind of dressing room to the Spanking Room. In it the chief piece of furniture was a large bed covered with a dark red velvet coverlet, while on the walls and ceiling were numerous mirrors.

Rose, pointing out to me the bed, said:

Be so good as to lie down there, on your back. I obeyed without asking for any explanation, knowing well that the good and skilful girl had something pleasant in store for us.

As soon as I had assumed the required position she turned up my shirt over my belly and pulled my trousers down to my knees.

'Oh! How big it is!' exclaimed Nora at once.

'Yes, I really believe it is bigger than Father Rustique's,' said Evelyn.

I could feel their warm breath caressing my flesh, so closely were they bending over me.

'Monsieur Quatrefois is very well made!' said Rose laughing. 'There is nothing exactly remarkable about him, but what you are examining with such interest is one of the finest specimens that I have ever seen!'

Human pride centres in all sorts of things and this compliment was not calculated to diminish mine. As a well known comedian used to sing in Paris.

> . . . *On a beau faire le malin,*
> *Ca vous fait tout de meme quelque chose!*

'Have you seen many?' asked Nora naively. Rose began to laugh:

'A fair number!' she admitted modestly. Then becoming suddenly grave and assuming the magisterial air which I have mentioned before, she continued.

'I will now show you in detail, young ladies, what a devil is! Perhaps it will make you wish to put it into hell. At any rate, I hope so. Now, watch – '

She took hold of my tool and held it upright, for in the position that I was lying in it was pointing straight up along my belly.

'What you see here, this bag which Miss Nora was tickling just now so nicely while she was whipping the gentleman contains the "testicles" or balls. Feel here, gently, quite gently. Do you feel the two balls?'

'Yes, yes! Oh how funny they feel!'

The little darlings were feeling me so delicately

and with such evident interest that it was almost more than I could stand.

'Well, these balls,' continued Rose, 'are called the seminal glands. It is in them that the juice of life is formed . . .'

'The juice of life?'

'Yes, or the semen, the liquid which when poured into the genital organs of a woman, produces the foetus, or the embryo child. This juice, or sperm, is the seed of life.'

'But how is it poured into . . . into what you were mentioning?' asked Evelyn.

'I will explain. When it is formed it is accumulated in a little reservoir situated here, between the cheeks of the bottom. Please to open your legs, sir!'

I obeyed at once and the instructing – and tickling! – finger was placed on my prostate.

'When the devil has been thrust right into hell, it is drawn out and then worked in and out, in and out, as no doubt you notice in the cinema room. The object of these movements is to rub the delicate soft surface of the weapon against the folds of the hot sheath in which it is plunged. This is intended to excite it and make it swell and stiffen as much as possible; do you follow?'

'Oh, yes, yes.'

'When it is thoroughly excited there takes place a natural contraction and a spasm which repeated several times, shoots out the seminal juice through this tube which you see swelling out so on the under side and through this little pink hole at the top. Then the juice is poured into the genital parts of the woman and baby is planted. Do you understand?'

'Yes, perfectly,' said Nora. 'But then, if this juice is to be shot out, the . . . the weapon must be in its sheath, Mademoiselle?'

'Oh! one can make it flow in other ways fortunately!'

'But then,' said Evelyn in her turn, 'if it is not properly placed a baby isn't made?'

Rose and I burst out laughing.

'If a baby was made every time that a man has this pleasure – for we experience just the same pleasure when we pour out our juice as you did just now at the end of your whipping – the world would soon be over-populated and people, for fear of having children, would indeed be unhappy!'

'Then . . . then? What can be done to make this juice flow?' asked Nora.

'Oh, that's quite simple,' said Rose. 'Instead of rubbing the weapon in its proper sheath one can rub it in some other way! Like this for instance; look! . . .'

She took hold of the middle of my tool and, slowly at first and then more quickly, began to frig me, half covering and uncovering the red head as she worked the skin up and down.

'Oh, how curious it is to see the head covered and uncovered like that!' said Evelyn.

'This head,' said Rose, 'is called the glans. And this soft supple skin which half covers it is called the foreskin. Now, Miss Evelyn, take hold of it gently and do as you have seen me do. It is called masturbating or, more commonly, frigging, but these are naughty words which must not be used in public, you understand! It is like the name "prick." Oh, there are plenty of them . . . plenty!'

'Oh, do tell them to us, Mademoiselle!' said the two girls both together.

'Don't know if I ought to . . .'

'Oh, yes, tell them,' I said. 'They want to know all we can teach them, don't you dearies?'

'Oh, yes, yes!' they exclaimed together.

'Very well, then! That great stiff thing that you have got hold of, Miss Evelyn, is properly called the penis but, more usually, a prick, cock, tool, etc., etc. But these are all nasty words and, for my part, I prefer to call it by affectionate names such as little mouse, doodle, etc., just as I call pussy, fanny, jewel, the famous sheath which we girls have and which is commonly called a cunt.'

'Oh! you are quite right,' said Evelyn excitedly. When I am married later on I shall ask my husband to put his little mouse into my little pussy and I do hope it really will be a little mouse rather than this great thing which I'm sure would never be able to get into my little pussy.'

Rose and I fairly roared at this, but in a moment Nora broke in shyly and blushing sweetly.

'But Mademoiselle, may we not see this juice which you have been telling us about? It would be so interesting to see it flow; and Uncle Jack has seen both of us . . . do . . . do what you made us do on the whipping chair!'

197

'Oh, yes, do let us, Mademoiselle!' chimed in Evelyn.

'And what do you say Monsieur Quatrefois?' asked Rose.

'I am quite willing,' said I. 'And I think their lesson would be incomplete without it.'

'Very well, then, young ladies, you shall now proceed to make your uncle "come" or "spend": but wait a minute!'

Rose went to a drawer and returned with a towel with which she covered me from my chin to my navel.

'Whatever is that for?' asked Evelyn.

'You will see in a minute,' said Rose, 'Now, Miss Evelyn, hold his prick straight up in the air and whatever happens don't let go of it . . . yes, that's right . . . Now place your other hand under the cheek of his bottom that is nearest you . . . And you, Miss Nora, place one of your hands under the other cheek, and with the tips of the fingers of the other hand just tickle up and down the shaft, touching that swelling tube with one of your fingers: do it as gently and as nicely as you can and tell me as soon as you feel his bottom begin to stiffen. Now are you both ready? Then begin . . .' Immediately I had the intense pleasure of feeling Nora's little fingers travelling softly up and down my straining tool and I watched with delight the eager and excited look on the face of each of the two charming girls. The delightful tickling of my prick soon began to take effect, and do what I would in my anxiety to prolong the pleasure as much as possible, the inevitable contractions of my bottom began to take place.

'Oh my cheek is beginning to stiffen!' said Evelyn.

'And so is mine!' said Nora.

'Ah, now he is beginning to feel just as you did at the end of your whipping,' broke in Rose. 'Now, Miss Nora, you see that drop of juice which is issuing from the top of his instrument?'

'Yes! Is that the . . . the seed of life that you were telling us about?'

'No, only its forerunner. Now, Miss, take that drop on the tip of your finger . . . Yes, that's right. Now rub your finger up and down just on the underneath part of his prick where the head joins the shaft. Yes, like that. Keep rubbing there and you'll see what happens!'

The action of the slippery tip of the finger on the most sensitive part of my tool was more than I could stand. My whole body stiffened and then with a jerk my love juice sluices were at last opened and I shot a stream of semen four or five feet into the air which came pattering down on to the towel just under my chin: another stream followed and another, each falling a little lower than the former till a long line covered the towel from top to bottom.

All the time that I was spending the two girls uttered exclamations of 'Oh! Oh! How wonderful! What a deluge! How delightful!', etc, etc.

'There,' said Rose, 'now you have frigged a man and made him spend and have learnt how his pleasure corresponds to ours, for you must have noticed that his body stiffened and jerked and how he panted and sighed just as you did when you were on the whipping chair. And now, that will do for the present. If you continued at once you would tire him out. I will now take you to a bedroom where, in view of what is to follow, certain ablutions will again be necessary. Monsieur Quatrefois will stay here and will, no doubt, be able to attend to himself: after that I will show you something else which I hope will interest you.'

7

THE CHAIR OF PLEASURE

The girls were back in a few minutes looking as bright and fresh as ever, and Rose at once led us into the room in which is the 'Chair of Pleasure.' This chair is a kind of arm-chair with a rather narrow seat and a padded back. On each side, instead of arms, are supports, also padded, on which the legs of the occupant can be comfortably hung. The height of the seat can be regulated at pleasure: so too, the back can be sloped more or less backwards and, when the legs of the 'subject' are placed on the supports, these can be opened at will thus causing the separation of the thighs.

Facing the chair, and fastened to the front legs by a kind of socket, is a sort of Saint-Andrew's cross, an X, and provided in the middle part of the lower arms with padded supports for the knees of the 'operator.' This X can be sloped forwards as is required.

The effect of the arrangement can be at once understood: when the girl is seated, with his legs raised and well separated, the man kneels down on the X which slopes forward and brings his mouth into the most convenient position for dealing with the treasures which are displayed before him. At the same time a second girl, lying under the chair, with her head between the lower arms of the X, finds herself admirably placed for an attack with lips and hands on the central regions of his body. On the floor were numerous cushions of all sizes and colours.

Rose moved the levers by which the action of the chair could be regulated and explained to us in detail the utility of the apparatus.

'But,' said Rose in conclusion, 'no explanation is anything like so satisfactory as really experiencing what I have been describing. Which of the young ladies will first take her place on the chair? . . .'

'Nora must!' decided Evelyn. 'I was the first to mount the whipping chair. But I will take her place afterwards for I want to know everything! Oh! Uncle Jack! How exciting it all is and how delightful to know about all these things.'

'You are not shocked, Evelyn?'

'Of course not . . . Why should I be? I know that these things are not for little girls, but I am aware also that women know all about them. So nothing shocks me. And besides, it doesn't prevent us from being modest, does it?'

'Certainly not, Evelyn. And when you and Nora are as learned as the most experienced women it doesn't follow that you need give yourselves to the first comer, eh?'

'Oh, no indeed,' said Nora with comic dignity. 'I'm sure we shall be most particular! . . .'

Rose laughed heartily at this and as I was gently urging Nora towards the chair in my impatience to enjoy her charms, she took me by the arm.

'One moment,' she said. 'If Nora is wise, she will make herself quite comfortable before sitting down on the chair. There is nothing so tiresome as finding one's clothes in the way!'

At these words Nora who was looking at her seemed to lose countenance.

She turned towards me, blushing delightfully, and I could see that a kind of shy fit had come over her.

'Nora, darling!' I said, pressing her softly in my arms. 'What is it! What's the matter?'

'Oh Uncle Jack!' she said. 'What does it mean? Does it mean that I am to undress?'

'Yes, of course, darling, that's just what Rose means. And, indeed, it's quite necessary: it's always done, you know. It's one of the things that you have to learn and I was waiting for Rose to teach it you.'

'Take off my clothes!' she murmured. 'Oh, no, really I couldn't!'

'Why not? After all that . . .'

'Uncle Jack,' broke in Evelyn, 'I understand Nora. Really she can't take off her clothes!'

'How absurd,' said Rose rather vexed. 'Why? You, both of you, had your petticoats up and your drawers down a few minutes ago, and the neighbouring regions fully exposed! . . .'

'Oh, it's not that!' said Evelyn impatiently. 'I

mean that Nora can't undress herself. She would never dare to, the little darling. I know her! Somebody will have to do it for her.'

'Shall I?' I suggested. 'Nora dear, shall I act as your "maid"?'

She pressed herself softly against me, covered with confusion and yielding herself to my embrace. Delightful combination of chastity and desire which, after all, is the breath of life!

'One word?' I begged. 'Say "yes," little sweetheart.'

'Ye . . . es,' she whispered in my ear.

How I should have devoured her rosy lips if we had been alone. But for the moment I had something better to do.

Delighted at having to carry out this charming task, I sat down on a chair and drew Nora between my knees as if she had been a little child. In spite of all she had been through she was still extremely shy and bashful.

She would submit to anything but would not undertake anything on her own. Such was the explanation of the little scene I have just described. Rose understood perfectly this frame of mind and did not ridicule it . . . girls always understood one another.

Nora covered her face with her hands and I set to work.

I unfastened her bodice down the back and gently removed it. At once I was aware of the delightful odor di femina which almost intoxicated me. Under the bodice, the pretty little camisole with its dainty ribbons disclosed the upper part of the back, breast and arms. The fair nest of the arm-pits appeared to me, and I could feel the snow-white breasts quiver under the edge of the richly laced chemise.

Having unfastened the skirt and slipped it down to her feet, the emotion which I felt was the most intense and delicate, and was increased by the fall of the soft petticoat which disclosed the splendid bottom enclosed in the pretty drawers which I have already described.

To be sure I had already seen this beautiful bottom, submitted to a tender whipping, but to uncover it thus by degrees and with my own hands was an additional pleasure.

I unbuttoned the drawers and slipped them down to her feet . . . Standing as she was between my legs with her back towards me, the splendid great twin globes almost pressed against my breast. The subtle perfume, formed of the natural odour and the scents which had been used in her ablutions, met my nostrils and increased my desire. I gently turned her towards me and, resting my hands on her bottom, which enabled me to feel, even through the thin chemise, its softness and its firm elasticity, I pressed the sweet girl to me.

'You are not afraid, my lovely one, are you?' I whispered. 'You know how much I already love and respect you?'

Yes. I uttered this word with all sincerity. I respected her as one respects everything that one loves.

What a poor sweet fluttering thing she was in my hands as I heard her murmur:

'Yes . . . Uncle Jack!'

I seized the lower part of her corset to undo the fastenings and my fingers felt the soft and exciting warmth of her immaculate belly. I removed the corset after having unfastened the suspenders to which the stockings were attached. In addition to these suspenders she was wearing a lovely pair of dark-blue ribbon garters, trimmed with loops and rose.

I decided to let her keep her stockings and shoes. A flapper, naked but for stockings and shoes, has always been my special delight.

I almost tore off the camisole and chemise, so eager was I to admire the marvels which I knew must be revealed and, indeed, I was not disappointed. Nora, stripped naked, was worthy of the chisel of a sculptor. Just a nice height, beautiful pink and white, just sufficiently plump without being too much so, she was made to perfection.

Her breasts were two sweet hills of snow tipped by a rosy nipple. Her supple waist grew smaller in harmony with her broad hips and her beautifully sloping loins, while her full and rounded thighs made one long to feel their pressure. One would have loved to die smothered by their soft but powerful grip.

Resting my hands on Nora's hips I turned her round so that I might enjoy the back view.

Here too all was perfection. Her lovely loins were marked by dimples which seemed to invite one's kisses, and the well developed globes, still red and burning from the effects of the whipping, stood out bold and exciting as though offering themselves to the most wanton caress unless it was to the equally maddening embraces of an elastic birch.

I rose and led Nora, still docile and a little trembling, to the chair.

'Sit down, sweetie!' I said, hardly able to speak so intense was my emotion.

She obeyed. Her beautiful blue eyes, so tender and trusting and slightly swimming as the result of her nervousness, gazed fondly into mine.

I bent over her and for a long moment I glued my lips to hers and as I pressed her naked body to me she made not the slightest effort to resist my hot embrace.

Then I took her dear legs and placed them in turn over the supports where they hung quite comfortably. This done I proceeded to strip, excusing myself to Evelyn and Rose who smilingly gave me a gesture of permission.

In a moment I was absolutely naked and I must confess that if Evelyn and Nora examined me with excited curiosity they raised not the slightest objection to the decidedly indecent appearance which I now presented, for my tool was standing as I think it never stood before. I knelt down on the padded supports of the lower arms of the X and leaning forward, moved towards the admirably displayed charms of my girl.

It is hardly necessary for me to enlarge on my own feelings at this moment and especially on my sensual emotions; the reader will easily imagine them . . . it is not often that one finds oneself in the position that I now occupied, my face between the well-opened thighs of a sixteen-year-old virgin, my eyes and lips within a few inches of her flower so pure, so fresh, so tempting and so fragrant and about to make her for the first time acquainted with the delights of a skilful gamahuche.

Placed as she was, Nora presented to me not only her anterior charms, but I was able to admire and handle her beautiful bottom, the greater part of which protruded beyond the narrow seat of the chair as well as the other tight little jewel, still more retiring and perhaps no less exciting to a man of real taste. When Nora found my head advancing between her thighs she made a little movement as though to withdraw her bottom.

'Little darling,' I murmured, 'don't be afraid!' I approached my lips to her pouting cunny and began by covering it and its surroundings with warm kisses.

So lovingly did I apply them they must have raised floods of pleasure in the very marrow of her being. There was soon evidence of this. Red and swollen like a delightful little cherry, the button which serves as the thermometer of feminine pleasure emerged from its grotto. I could not help taking it softly in my lips and sucking it as if it had been a delicious bonbon and tickling it keenly with my quick and pointed tongue.

At once a perfect frenzy of delight seemed to take possession of Nora.

With her hands gripping the sides of the chair,

her breasts quivering with the most intense emotion, her belly undulating with the spasms of the aproaching love-fit, she stretched herself out on the chair and, in my hands, which had not ceased to caress and fondle them, I felt the cheeks of her bottom begin to quiver and then to stiffen and stiffen till they were as hard as the muscles of a wrestler at the moment of his supreme effort.

Thanks to the position of her head, which was resting on the back of the chair, I was able to watch her lovely face while still continuing my caress. Her lips were slightly open and contracted by the voluptuous agony she was experiencing; her half-closed eyes seemed to turn up to heaven as if she was about to swoon away and inarticulate words were panted out.

'Oh! Ooooh! Go on! Oh, it's delicious. Oh, I must . . . Oh! Aaaah; Go on! Go on! Oh! I shall die!'

She pressed herself with all her strength against my lips. Sometimes as the result of her movements my chin was buried between the powerful cheeks of her bottom in a way that almost drove me mad with desire. Slowly, and using all my skill, I tickled with the tip of my hot moist tongue the delicious little button which I was pressing between my lips, and I was extracting sobs of pleasure and sighs of delight from my little darling when suddenly a great shudder of emotion shook me from head to foot.

A new source of pleasure, more distinctly personal, had just been communicated to me. In a moment I realised what it was. Following the instructions of Rose, who had placed some cushions conveniently for her, Evelyn was lying down underneath me in such a position that her face was just on a level with my stiff-standing prick. And there, somewhat timidly at first, she was caressing my balls, my tool, my bottom, and my thighs while her lips softly kissed the red head of my throbbing weapon!

Kneeling by her side, Rose was minutely directing the operations. She was showing her how pleasant and effective it is to gently tickle the bottom and just underneath the balls, and was teaching her to roll them delicately in her soft hands, to frig my prick with one hand while she tickled me with the other, and finally to kiss my balls and prick and to pass her tongue round and round the red head and with the tip to tickle the supersensitive little thread which joins the foreskin to the gland.

I was able to feel delightfully how perfectly Evelyn carried out all her instructions, while all the time I continued to suck Nora's little rosebud and to cover her charms with my fondest attentions.

I knew that Rose was coming to the end of her lesson when I felt the head of my prick pressed and sucked by two hot lips, while a slippery tongue played up and down and all round it. At the same time two hands continued to fondle and stroke my balls and bottom, each one being differently employed. I heard Rose murmur as she guided the delicate fingers between the cheeks of my bottom.

'This we call "*pattes d'araignée*." Give me your finger . . . here. Yes, that's it . . . Push it well in. It's an intimate caress which they all love!'

I felt Evelyn's finger pressed slowly into my back entrance and the sensation which it caused me almost made me spend at once. It was only by the exercise of the utmost restraint that I avoided doing so and this because I was determined to reserve myself for what I felt sure was to come afterwards. Meanwhile Nora, who had not the same reasons for restraining herself, had fairly let herself go. To use the words of the psalms 'her soul melted within her.' For the third time that afternoon her love-sluices were opened and she poured into my delightful lips a copious draught of the essence of her being. For a few moments she lay panting and quivering, her soft white belly undulating with the gradually subsiding spasm.

I, with my eyes closed and my cheeks resting on Nora's fair downy-bush, abandoned myself to Evelyn's maddening caresses but always with the intention of stopping just short of the climax. I was therefore not sorry when at a sign from Rose she ceased her ministrations and rose to her feet. I did the same and took her in my arms.

'Oh, Evelyn, you darling!' I murmured. 'What don't I owe you for the delightful time you have been giving me?'

'Well,' said Rose. 'You can repay her in kind! And Miss Nora will return the compliment which you have been paying her! That's only fair, isn't it?'

'Quite fair! . . .'

211

'Undress Miss Evelyn then, and I'm sure you won't find the task at all unpleasant!'

I began to laugh and, drawing Evelyn between my knees as I had done in the case of Nora, I asked her:

'May I, darling?'

She smiled shyly at me and whispered:

'Yes, Uncle Jack!'

How sweet and lovely she was! My hands trembled as they unfastened her bodice and then the waist of her skirt, which I removed as well as her petticoat, and again I experienced the sensual pleasure which the sight of a pretty girl in corset and drawers always rouses in me.

Stripping Evelyn was an absolute delight to me. When she was quite naked, as I carried my mind back to our meeting on the boat and then thought what she was to me at this moment, I felt a strong desire to kneel before her and kiss in adoration her feet, her knees, her thighs and the whole of her fresh young body, so full of mystery and so radiant with virgin charm.

And did so.

She hardly defended herself, happy, in reality, at receiving a homage which she knew to be fully deserved.

My lips wandered over her beautiful body, arousing little quivers of pleasure wherever they passed and I should have continued the delightful sport if Rose had not interrupted me saying:

'Come now; get to work. You will be able to kiss her more conveniently in a moment! . . .'

I myself placed Evelyn on the chair. Oh! the

lingering caresses on her bottom, still hot and blushing from its whipping, as I did so. I placed her legs on the arms which Rose opened wide apart and I knelt down on the X which at once moved towards her.

Beautiful as Nora is, Evelyn is not one whit less so. She is not quite so well built and is less white but her skin is as fine, and if her forms are less plump they are more graceful and more full of nerves which makes them equally alluring. To sum up – and now even more than then I am in a position to state this – when I am with Nora I think that no one can equal her in beauty and attraction. When I am with Evelyn I no longer think of Nora, and I find the dark and dazzling Evelyn the most intoxicating of creatures.

Some day perhaps I will describe their essential differences more accurately but now I will content myself with saying that Evelyn is all energy and activity, while at the same time being just as passionately voluptuous as Nora, who, for her part, would rather be passive and tenderly submissive to refined caresses.

For the moment I was in adoration before Evelyn's sanctuary of love.

A fine thick dark brown bush, as curly and soft as astrakhan, sheltered in its shady folds the fountain at which I was about to quench my greedy thirst.

The whole lovely body of the charming girl was quivering with desire. I kissed her thighs and belly, and then my active tongue sought out and roused from its grotto the little rosy god who

213

issued forth swollen and delicious, and allowed himself to be seized by my eager lips.

My hands fondled and pressed her thighs and marble bottom, while my tongue softly tickled the little sensitive button.

Evelyn raised herself on the arms of the chair into almost an upright position: her powerful thighs gripped my cheeks and held me prisoner in their fond embrace. She threw her head back, her neck was arched, and from her half-opened mouth, a very nest for kisses, issued exclamations and sobs and sighs of pleasure. Then the sweet girl uttered a cry of delight as her fountains were opened and a stream of the dew of love was poured into my eager mouth, for she had locked her thighs round my neck and was pressing her little cunt to my lips in a way which almost smothered me.

The mere memory of this, the first love-grip that she ever gave me, almost drives me mad! Evelyn had come much more quickly than Nora. This is always the case with dark girls, so Rose assured me and my experience agrees with hers.

Meanwhile I had been aware that Nora had not been carrying out her part of the programme as Evelyn – who was now lying back in the chair resting comfortably – had done and I asked Rose to give her the necessary instructions. Nora lay down under me and in a moment I felt her hands stroking me and her lips and tongue sucking and tickling in the most delightful manner. It was perfectly plain to me that she was doing her level best to make me spend again, and it was with the utmost difficulty that I restrained myself from pouring a torrent of the seed of life into her hot juicy little mouth. The moment came when I could resist no more and jerking my throbbing tool from between her lips I stood up, panting violently. Nora also got up and looked at me with distressed surprise.

'Was I hurting, uncle dear?' she asked softly.

Great tears were actually gleaming in her beautiful eyes. I took her naked body in my arms and pressed her madly to me, and as I did so the pressure of my prick against her soft belly made her tremble with passion and again almost caused me to give way.

'Hurt me, darling!' I said in transport. 'How could you hurt me, my sweet, my love? No, far from it . . . But let me explain.'

I drew Evelyn to me also and made each of them sit on one of my knees, and the sensation of the soft fat naked bottoms of these two delightful flappers on my thighs was such as I can hardly describe.

'Both of you urge me by your loving caresses to spend just as both of you have just spent, but I don't want to do it again yet.'

'Why?' they both asked together.

'Because, you dears, a man's prick has neither the strength nor the staying powers of your little cunnies. When a man spends he shoots out a stream of love-juice as you know, don't you?'

'Yes, Uncle Jack.'

'Well! Each time that he shoots it out it is very exhausting for him, and when he has done it three or four times, and not many men, can do this, his prick becomes small, quite small, and it is no easy matter to rouse it!'

'But Uncle Jack,' said Evelyn laughing, 'you have only . . . spent once and here is your . . . your prick getting quite, quite small as you say!'

As she said this she took hold of my tool which, really fatigued by its intense nervous strain, had lowered its head and failed to come to life again even at the touch of her dainty hand.

'Oh what a pity!' exclaimed Nora really sadly. 'What is to be done? I should so like to see you "come" again.'

I must confess that I was highly amused to see how well the two girls remembered the lesson that Rose had given them and how quickly and naturally they were beginning to use the 'naughty' words of love, but it is my experience that this is always so directly after a girl has been gamahuched by a man and has had his tool in her mouth. Nothing so quickly makes them on perfectly intimate terms, not even the genuine fuck.

'And Rose, who has had no pleasure at all!' exclaimed Evelyn. 'Oh, no, it's not fair! We really must find some means of making them both happy.'

'There is a very simply way,' said Rose. 'Monsieur Quatrefois – as he has only shown his power once – must justify his name and at the same time give you a living representation of what you saw in the cinema room. He will be Father

Rustique and I will undertake the part of Alibech! . . .

'How charming of you, Rose,' I said sincerely. 'But I must confess that it was with the intention of making this suggestion that I have been reserving myself!'

'That's very charming of you too. The young ladies won't be jealous I hope?'

'My dear girls,' I said, 'you possess a "capital" which a proper young lady ought to keep intact till her marriage. This capital would disappear if I introduced my devil into your little hell, do you understand?'

'Not quite,' said Nora.

'Oh, I do!' said Evelyn blushing divinely. 'If Uncle Jack did as he says, he would make something disappear; I don't quite know what, but it is called our virginity. Isn't that what you mean, uncle?'

'Yes,' said I, 'that's exactly it. This something is a very thin membrane which is called the "hymen." When this membrane is pierced, which always happens the first time that a prick is inserted into her pussy, the girl is no longer a virgin. When she is married her husband might notice this.'

'Oh, I understand now!' said Nora eagerly. 'But then . . .'

She seemed uneasy, blushed crimson and was silent.

'But then what?' asked Evelyn impatiently . . . Out with it, Nora.'

'But then . . . Uncle Jack's tongue . . .'

We all three burst out laughing which increased Nora's confusion and Evelyn said:

'I'm not very learned in these matters, but I know all the same that there's a considerable difference between the little end of a tongue and a great big prick! And besides, if there wasn't I should not be a virgin either! . . .'

'And no girl of your age would be; I asserted boldly. That little operation which I have performed on you, darlings, is just what your young friends of the Lesbian Society do to one another!'

'Really,' said Evelyn, evidently a little vexed; 'do they do all that?'

'All that? Certainly not! Only a part, the kisses and the caresses with the finger and tongue, but they have no convenient arm-chair, and above all no man to play with and be fondled by. I feel certain that probably not one of them has ever seen a stiff-standing prick, and still less handled it and kissed it. So you see you are much more learned than they are, and when the time comes for you to be admitted into this select society you will be able to "epater" them in many ways without letting them know how you have acquired your wide experience.'

At this they were highly delighted and Evelyn continued:

'Then, Uncle Jack, you must be happy again and make dear Mademoiselle Rose happy too, who has been so kind and useful to us.'

'There's nothing I should like better,' said Rose laughing, 'but really Monsieur Quatrefois is not in the necessry condition. See how humble his devil is!'

'Oh, the tiresome thing!' said Nora, shaking her finger at it.

'What's to be done?' said Evelyn. 'I wish Nora and I could rouse it up. How could we do it, Mademoiselle Rose?'

'Oh,' said Rose, 'there are many ways, but I think strong measures will have to be taken judging by its present condition. A birching might do it . . .'

'A birching?' said Nora.

'Yes, certainly! It's one of the most effective ways of rousing the feelings as you yourself know, Miss Nora, and there are certain caresses . . . Oh, but wait a moment. I have an idea. Tell me, Monsieur, do the young ladies know what a 69 is?'

'No, I feel certain they don't,' I answered. A thrill of pleasure passed through me at the mere idea of what was in store for me thanks to the inventive powers of the excellent Rose.

'Very well then,' said she, 'we will show them how to do it.'

'It's perfectly delightful,' I said, in answer to an enquiring glance which Evelyn and Nora gave me. 'It's one of the most intimate and refined caresses . . .'

And I added coolly and with an assurance which surprised myself:

'It's much used in the best society. You'll see how delicious it is. Which of you will be my partner?'

'Oh, I will, I will,' they said both together. Little darlings, they were indeed anxious to know everything!

They both flung their naked bodies on mine at the same moment and I could not help laughing at their naughty eagerness.

'Listen,' I said. 'You are both of you perfectly sweet and I love you both absolutely equally, so it's rather difficult to make a choice. Shall we draw lots?'

'Oh, yes, but how shall we manage it?'

'Very easily. Come here, Evelyn, and leave me to manage it!'

I took her to a corner of the room and, putting my left arm round her supple waist, bent her down as if I was about to smack her.

'What are you going to do?' she panted.

'Don't be afraid! . . . Now, Rose, turn the other way. Tell me now in which charming little nest my finger is lodged! Wait! If you guess right it shall be Evelyn, if wrong, Nora.'

'Oh, splendid!' cried Rose, bursting with laughter: 'you really are grand at inventing games for polite society. . . . Are you ready?'

'Uncle Jack! . . . Oh, Uncle Jack! . . .' sighed Evelyn, overcome with confusion.

'Yes, now I'm ready!' I cried.

'Well! Your naughty finger is in the tight little back entrance! . . .'

'You are right,' I said, slowly withdrawing my finger and allowing Evelyn to rise.

'I'm beginning to understand you,' said Rose. 'See, young ladies, if 69 isn't a powerful caress

220

since the mere idea that he is going to take part in it makes his devil begin to raise his head at once! . . .'

As a matter of fact it was not only the idea of the caress in question but how could I have remained insensible to the subtle charm of the little game which I had just played with Evelyn.

I arranged some cushions on the floor and stretched myself, comfortably on them on my back. Evelyn then took up her position in accordance with Rose's instructions.

She was resting slightly on her knees right across my chest with her belly bent down and pressed close to mine. My parts were thus most conveniently placed for the action both of her hands and lips, while, owing to the wide stretch of her legs, my face was plunged between her thighs and the well-opened cheeks of her bottom. A little wriggle on her part and I felt her sweet cunny pressed upon my lips. Then I felt my prick buried in her soft mouth which at once began to work up and down, while her now skilful fingers tickled under my balls and the surrounding neighbourhood in the most delightful fashion.

I returned her attentions in my very best style. My tongue travelled up and down, in and out of the virgin lips and my hands fondled and patted the beautiful globes placed just above my eyes.

Floods of pleasure passed through me and I was beginning to feel that I should not much longer be able to restrain the bursting of the dykes, when, in answer to a brisk attack on her litle clitoris, I felt the darling tremble and then stiffen and a stream of love-juice bathed my lips and face.

The violence of her love-fit, thus experienced for the fourth time that afternoon, caused her to withdraw her lips from my tool, and just in time to save my own eruption.

Rose at once lifted the panting girl off me and placed her on a chair to rest. Then stooping over me she examined the state of my devil and said:

'You are not quite ready; Miss Nora must complete the work which her young friend has so well begun. Come Miss Nora . . . No, wait one moment while I just pass a sponge over this prick which you will very soon be able to bring to a fine condition.' She hastened to perform this grateful task and at the same time handed me a towel with which I removed the very evident traces of Evelyn's recent emotion.

'Now, Nora darling!' I said, 'it's for you to complete the work.'

In a moment she was in position.

I have not the slightest hesitation in saying that each of us did our very best to make it as pleasant as possible for the other; each, I believe, was more bent on giving to me the very acme of lovemaking.

So delightfully did she suck me that I am certain she was hoping to make me come in her mouth, for she had placed her hands under my bottom and as she felt the cheeks stiffen her lips and tongue became more active as if she knew that her desire was about to be fulfilled. And I only just managed to avert the catastrophe.

For if I was roused to the highest pitch of pleasure, so was my little partner, and suddenly her fountains were opened and she too knew, for the fourth time like Evelyn, the pleasure of a luscious spend.

Immediately Rose, who was keenly on the watch and who knew that now I must be in perfect condition for her purpose, pulled the dear girl off me and pushed her into an arm-chair.

'And now,' said she with undisguised joy, 'it's my turn. Monsieur Quatrefois, you must justify your name, mustn't you?'

'I'll do my very best, my pretty Rose,' I said; 'and if I don't succeed with you I should not be able to do so with anyone, for you have everything to please me and make me happy!'

8

THREE STORIES, THREE VICTORIES!

We did not take the trouble to go into another room where there was a bed. We could manage very well where we were.

In a moment Rose had stripped herself as naked as the rest of us.

Two cushions, to the right and left, those on which we had just performed our delightful 69, served as seats for Evelyn and Nora.

'Come and sit here,' I said to them. 'You will be quite close to us and will be able to see even better than in the cinema room how the devil is put into hell!'

They were evidently highly excited at the idea of what they were about to witness.

'Oh! How amusing it will be. I shall watch as closely as ever I can!' said Evelyn.

'And may we feel?' asked Nora.

'Certainly!' I said. 'And if by chance you notice any momentary weakening on the part of the devil, don't hesitate to rouse him by any means in your power; you pretty well know how to do that now, I think!'

'That will be capital,' said Rose. 'And for our part we'll do our best to put in practice all the instructions we have given . . . But as we are still concerned with the story of the Devil in Hell, we will try to make three stories of it, that will not be beyond your powers, Monsieur Quatrefois?'

'I will do my best, my pretty one!'

'The first . . . then: we will represent it in the most ordinary manner. Get up, lazy one, and let me take your place. You shall have the honour of mounting me.'

She took my place, settling herself comfortably with one cushion under her head, another under back and a third under her bottom.

Rose, as will easily be imagined, was a charming specimen of Parisian beauty.

She was dark, with great big eyes, cheeks as red and soft as the skin of a peach, a small rosy mouth and a pretty little nose. Her breasts were firm and well developed and beautifully tipped with pink rose-buds which at this moment were standing as stiff as little pricks. Her waist was small and her thighs and bottom really magnificent — I had chosen her as my special 'friend' on account of this peculiarity — while her feet and hands were worthy of a duchess. I was always delighted to be with her, for her whims and manners were most attractive and she had a peculiarly charming way both of giving and — what to me is equally important — of receiving pleasure.

She opened her thighs; I knelt between them

and then stretched myself along her belly: as I did so she placed one arm round my waist and with her other hand began to stroke and pat my bottom encouraging me to the attack. Very slowly, so that my two little flappers might see every detail of the operation, I thrust my devil into the delightful hell which was so conveniently placed to receive him.

Immediately Rose folded her legs across mine and gripped me more tightly. Her pretty mouth took possession of mine, her hands clasped my bottom and I slipped mine under hers in order to press her more closely to me. Her hips began to undulate, inviting me to a similar movement, and for a moment we rubbed ourselves together as if we had desired to form but one body. As her pleasure rose she plunged her hot little tongue into my mouth and seemed to be trying to suck my very life from me.

'Now, do it!' she said suddenly with intense passion.

I saw that she was ready and I began to fuck her at once. Slowly at first, and by degrees more rapidly, my bottom rose and fell with firm and steady thrust.

Suddenly Rose arched up her loins and seemed to support herself only on her bottom and head, her nails dug themselves into my stiffly contracted cheeks and with panting sobs and sighs she spent and spent and spent while at the same moment I poured into her a perfect torrent of my love-juice.

For a short time we lay motionless, panting in

one another's arms, then I raised myself on my knees.

My prick was still in full erection: a great drop of seed issued from its head and fell upon the carpet.

Evelyn and Nora, much moved as their glowing cheeks and sparkling eyes plainly testified, were examining myself and my tool in turn.

'Uncle Jack!' murmured Evelyn, 'you haven't hurt yourself?'

'Quite the contrary!' I sighed. 'My pleasure has been intense.'

'More intense than ours was?'

'Much more. You will understand it when you make love in this way.'

'And that won't be till we are married! Oh, what a pity! Don't you think so Evelyn?' said Nora.

'Yes, that I do!' replied Evelyn. 'Oh, Uncle Jack, is it necessary to carry out the agreement that you made?'

'Yes, dear,' I answered, 'it certainly is today, but I don't see why we should have any such agreement on some future occasion if you are both agreeable?'

'Oh, that would be splendid!' they both exclaimed together.

Was that 'future occasion' ever to be realised? Ah, that would be revealing secrets, which I never do!

'So the young ladies are satisfied with what they have seen?' asked Rose.

'Very satisfied!' I replied laughing.

'But I'm not!' said Rose.

'Why?'

'Why? Because I want to have two more turns and even then I shall be "one down" on the young ladies.'

I laughed heartily at this, not being aware that among her other English accomplishments Rose had picked up the language of golf.

'Very well, Rose,' I said, 'how shall we narrate the second story?'

'How?' said she. 'Shall we do it "dog-fashion" as you call it, or as we say "enlevrette"? How will that suit you?'

'Splendidly, Rose, as it's with you that I'm to do it.'

'Oh!' said she laughing.' 'You are becoming as polite as a Frenchman!'

She knelt down on a cushion and then bent forward on to her elbows, and I got into position behind her.

For anyone who, like myself, is an intense admirer of a fine bottom, there is no more delightful position than this. The mere contact of the marble cheeks of the girl you are about to enjoy, as your belly and thighs press against her bottom, is sufficient to make you capable of your best performance. And in addition, this position permits of your weapon being buried to the very hilt in its warm sheath, which, in itself, is no slight pleasure.

I was just feeling for this sheath when an idea occurred to me and I took Nora's little hand.

'Put it in for me, darling!' I said, 'you yourself put my great mouse into Rose's little pussy!'

With a merry laugh, stooping forward, she felt for my prick and took hold of it and as she did so her splendid pig-tail dropped off her back and fell on mine and tickled it delightfully.

'And you, Evelyn, give me a nice little whipping: smack my bottom for me gently, and, Nora, when you have lodged my prick, tickle my balls for me in a way that you do so delightfully . . . Oh you darlings, how sweet you are to me!'

And, indeed, could anything be more delightful than my situation at that moment.

My hands were fondling and stroking Rose's belly, bottom and thighs and as I could not profit by her lips, for she was resting her face on her hands and her forehead on the cushion, I made up for it by raining hot kisses, now on the soft warm mouth of Nora, now on the glowing lips of Evelyn . . . Meanwhile I was fucking Rose with all the vigour that I could put into it. Soon I felt her bottom quiver and contract, her loins rose and fell in time with my thrusts and she turned her head backwards. Then she began to sigh and pant and utter little cries of pleasure and exclamations of joy, and in her excitement she dropped into her own language:

'Ah! . . . Ah . . . Encore! Fort! Fort! Ah! Que c'est bon! Ah! . . . Je! . . . Ah! Arrh . . .'

She writhed like a serpent. And her tight cunt and powerful bottom and thighs seemed to press and milk my cock like a squeezing hand.

All the time Nora continued to tickle and

stroke me and once or twice, as I heaved my bottom up, her fingers closed round my straining prick evidently with the object of testing its condition which, she must have been pleased to find, left nothing to be desired. At the same time Evelyn continued to smack me, paying, as I noticed, equal attention to each cheek of my bottom. It was not long before the crisis was again reached and this time also we came at the same moment.

I was so pleased with the success of this second bout that — finding that my powers were by no means exhausted — I at once suggested that we should enter on our third course.

'And how are we to relate our third story, Rose dear?'

'Shall we do a "St George"?' said she, showing all her teeth. 'I am very fond of this position and it will be a bit of rest to you!'

'Oh!' I answered: 'I'm by no means tired, I can assure you.'

I lay down on my back and stretching out my legs, the charming girl knelt astride of my body: then she took hold of my prick and, holding it upright, placed the head just within the lips of her now well-oiled little cunt.

I held out to her my hands which she took and pressed passionately and then, making use of them for a support, she gradually lowered herself till my tool was buried in her up to the very hilt. There then she rested for a few moments, and then began to glide slowly up and down. She continued the movement for some time, and for both of us the sensation was delightful.

Quite calmly Rose looked in turn at Evelyn and Nora, who were watching the operation with the utmost interest and excitement.

'Watch well how I'm doing it!' she said. 'It's quite simple as you see. And it's one of the operations most appreciated by men. By nature, I think they are lazy and they like to make us girls take all the trouble to please them. Do this to your husbands when you are married and you will see how pleased they will be. If by any chance they ask you who taught you this game, you had better inform them that they have no right to be so inquisitive; but at the same time you may tell them that it was your teacher of philosophy, a very smart young lady! . . . That will certainly please them!'

'Rose,' I murmured, fearing that she was carrying her irony really too far. 'Do be sensible!'

'Am I not so, dear friend? Why, I philosophise at the same time as I continue to make things extremely pleasant for us both.'

She continued her steady up and down movement and the soft juicy rubbing of her tight little cunt on my now throbbing prick was indeed delightful.

Again she turned her head towards Evelyn and Nora, who hardly understood what she was driving at and, this time quite seriously, resumed.

'Yes, young ladies, one ought to teach girls the art of giving pleasure to men. Yes, there ought to be classes for love-making as there are for drawing and music. Be assured that this counts as much in life – and indeed more – than anything else. One of the first principles ought to be this: "Love-making is not brutal." In the act of love everything should be gentle, deliberate, and well thought out. Even a kiss idly given is not fit to be called a kiss. And in all caresses it is the same. Do you understand?'

'Well said, Rose!' I exclaimed. 'Those are very sound sentiments!'

Rose pressed my hands more tenderly and, bending her knees well under her, she sat right down on me with my prick buried in her cunt, and her splendid bottom resting on my thighs. There she continued her movement, only instead of being rubbed against my thighs, her bush against my bush, her belly against mine. Her stiffened breasts stood out like marble and yet trembled with pleasure. Her mouth opened and panting sighs issued from her ruby lips. I too was ready; and as suddenly she stiffened all over and then, arching her back and loins and throwing herself back in my arms, she for the third time opened her sluices of love, I too gave her a final dose of my seed of life.

For a few moments she remained hanging in my arms as one dead; then with a smile she rose from me and led Evelyn and Nora away to a dressing-room saying, as she left:

'You will know where to find what you want?' I made a sign of assent and, picking up my clothes, retired to a bath-room by the little passage which connected it with the room of the Chair of Pleasure.

EPILOGUE

A little later, the two girls and I, quite recovered from our exertions, met in Madame R's private room. I had handed Rose, with a request to give a part of it to Marie, a handsome present which I think it will be agreed she had fully earned. Discreetly, so that Evelyn and Nora might not notice it, I paid Madame R according to the terms that we had arranged, and then, seated in comfortable arm-chairs, we talked for little before taking our leave.

'So the young ladies are pleased with the little visit they have paid us?' asked Madame.

'Quite, I think,' I answered, 'are you not, girls?'

'Oh, quite pleased,' said Evelyn.

'It has been absolutely delightful,' added Nora.

'I quite agree,' said I. 'Everything has gone off most successfully; you have, I think, had a decidedly pleasant time and have acquired much extremely useful knowledge, thanks to the excellent lesson of our charming little Rose; and who will profit by these lessons? Your husbands will later on when you are married!'

They blushed prettily at the idea that one day they would have a husband whom they would be able to make use of, each according to her own taste.

'And besides,' I added, 'before you are married there are others who will benefit by your newly acquired science. These are the members of the Lesbian Society to whom you will be able to impart much information which, but for you, they would never know.'

We took leave of the worthy Madame R who in her innermost heart, was delighted at the evident pleasure and gratitude of the two well-born young English flappers.

'Mascottes they entered my house and mascottes they leave it,' she whispered in my ear as she led us down-stairs. 'And yet they have had some decidedly interesting experiences, the little dears! Well, it has been an adventure which is altogether out of the common! At any rate it has been most profitable to my establishment!'

I took my two 'nieces' back to their school in a taxi and Madame X thanked me for having been good enough to escort them.

'Ah,' she said, 'if all guardians and visitors were so conscientious I should not be so anxious, I can assure you.'

'Madame,' I said, 'I was in charge of two precious young persons and when I undertake any responsibility I like to carry it through. So can I take Evelyn and her friend Nora out again next week or, if I am not able to do that, when I next return to Paris?'

'Whenever you like, monsieur; I shall be only too pleased to entrust them to you, the dear girls!'

She looked affectionately at the young ladies and added:

'At this age they are so pure! Isn't it natural that one should do one's utmost to avoid the slightest strain on their innocence? . . .'

I bowed my agreement and with a last farewell to Evelyn and Nora, sad at our parting but smiling affectionately at me all the same, I made my way back to my hotel.

MORE EROTIC CLASSICS FROM CARROLL & GRAF

- ☐ Anonymous/ALTAR OF VENUS $3.95
- ☐ Anonymous/AUTOBIOGRAPHY OF A FLEA $3.95
- ☐ Anonymous/THE CELEBRATED MISTRESS $3.95
- ☐ Anonymous/CONFESSIONS OF AN ENGLISH MAID $3.95
- ☐ Anonymous/CONFESSIONS OF EVELINE $3.95
- ☐ Anonymous/COURT OF VENUS $3.95
- ☐ Anonymous/DANGEROUS AFFAIRS $3.95
- ☐ Anonymous/THE DIARY OF MATA HARI $3.95
- ☐ Anonymous/DOLLY MORTON $3.95
- ☐ Anonymous/THE EDUCATION OF A MAIDEN $3.95
- ☐ Anonymous/THE EROTIC READER $3.95
- ☐ Anonymous/THE EROTIC READER II $3.95
- ☐ Anonymous/THE EROTIC READER III $4.50
- ☐ Anonymous/FANNY HILL'S DAUGHTER $3.95
- ☐ Anonymous/FLORENTINE AND JULIA $3.95
- ☐ Anonymous/A LADY OF QUALITY $3.95
- ☐ Anonymous/LENA'S STORY $3.95
- ☐ Anonymous/THE LIBERTINES $4.50
- ☐ Anonymous/LOVE PAGODA $3.95
- ☐ Anonymous/THE LUSTFUL TURK $3.95
- ☐ Anonymous/MADELEINE $3.95
- ☐ Anonymous/A MAID'S JOURNEY $3.95
- ☐ Anonymous/MAID'S NIGHT IN $3.95
- ☐ Anonymous/THE OYSTER $3.95
- ☐ Anonymous/THE OYSTER II $3.95
- ☐ Anonymous/THE OYSTER III $4.50
- ☐ Anonymous/PARISIAN NIGHTS $4.50
- ☐ Anonymous/PLEASURES AND FOLLIES $3.95
- ☐ Anonymous/PLEASURE'S MISTRESS $3.95
- ☐ Anonymous/PRIMA DONNA $3.95
- ☐ Anonymous/ROSA FIELDING: VICTIM OF LUST $3.95
- ☐ Anonymous/SATANIC VENUS $4.50
- ☐ Anonymous/SECRET LIVES $3.95
- ☐ Anonymous/THREE TIMES A WOMAN $3.95

☐	Anonymous/VENUS DISPOSES	$3.95
☐	Anonymous/VENUS IN PARIS	$3.95
☐	Anonymous/VENUS UNBOUND	$3.95
☐	Anonymous/VENUS UNMASKED	$3.95
☐	Anonymous/VICTORIAN FANCIES	$3.95
☐	Anonymous/THE WANTONS	$3.95
☐	Anonymous/A WOMAN OF PLEASURE	$3.95
☐	Anonymous/WHITE THIGHS	$4.50
☐	Perez, Faustino/LA LOLITA	$3.95
☐	van Heller, Marcus/ADAM & EVE	$3.95
☐	van Heller, Marcus/THE FRENCH WAY	$3.95
☐	van Heller, Marcus/THE HOUSE OF BORGIA	$3.95
☐	van Heller, Marcus/THE LOINS OF AMON	$3.95
☐	van Heller, Marcus/ROMAN ORGY	$3.95
☐	van Heller, Marcus/VENUS IN LACE	$3.95
☐	Villefranche, Anne-Marie/FOLIES D'AMOUR	$3.95
	Cloth	$14.95
☐	Villefranche, Anne-Marie/JOIE D'AMOUR	$3.95
	Cloth	$13.95
☐	Villefranche, Anne-Marie/ MYSTERE D'AMOUR	$3.95
☐	Villefranche, Anne-Marie/PLAISIR D'AMOUR	$3.95
	Cloth	$12.95
☐	Von Falkensee, Margarete/BLUE ANGEL NIGHTS	$3.95
☐	Von Falkensee, Margarete/BLUE ANGEL SECRETS	$4.50

Available from fine bookstores everywhere or use this coupon for ordering.

Carroll & Graf Publishers, Inc., 260 Fifth Avenue, N.Y., N.Y. 10001

Please send me the books I have checked above. I am enclosing
$_____ (please add $1.00 per title to cover postage and
handling.) Send check or money order—no cash or C.O.D.'s
please. N.Y. residents please add 8¼% sales tax.

Mr/Mrs/Ms _____
Address _____
City _____ State/Zip _____
Please allow four to six weeks for delivery.